D0894846

THE
TWO WRONG HALVES
OF
Ruby
Taylor

ALSO BY AMANDA PANITCH

The Trouble with Good Ideas

It's My Party and I Don't Want to Go

This book is for Merrilee Heifetz,
literary agent of valor.

THE
TWO WRONG HALVES
OF
RUBY
TAYLOR

AMANDA PANITCH

Roaring Brook Press
New York

Published by Roaring Brook Press
Roaring Brook Press is a division of Holtzbrinck Publishing Holdings
Limited Partnership
120 Broadway, New York, NY 10271 • mackids.com

Our books may be purchased in bulk for promotional, educational, or
business use. Please contact your local bookseller or the Macmillan
Corporate and Premium Sales Department at (800) 221-7945 ext. 5442
or by email at MacmillanSpecialMarkets@macmillan.com.
Library of Congress Cataloging-in-Publication Data is available.

First edition, 2022
Book design by Veronica Mang
Printed in the United States of America by LSC Communications,
Harrisonburg, Virginia

ISBN 978-1-250-24513-7
1 3 5 7 9 10 8 6 4 2

CHAPTER ONE

IF YOU'VE NEVER DROPPED AN entire pot of your grandmother's famous matzah balls down the stairs, let me tell you: You are much luckier than I am. I stood frozen near the top of the basement staircase, my eyes wide with horror as I watched the matzah balls tumble from step to step as if trying to march back toward the basement fridge and pantry shelves.

Did you know that matzah balls bounce?

The sound each ball made on the dusty wood was a sick *squelch*, much like the sound an eyeball would make if you dropped it from a great height. Matzah balls are a little like eyeballs, actually. They squish in your hand in a similar way, and they are about the same size, though eyeballs are much less delicious. Or so I assume. I have never actually eaten an eyeball.

Mr. Zammit warned us against it. The whole reason I know the exact squishiness of an eyeball is because we'd just finished dissecting cow eyeballs in our sixth-grade science class. "These have been soaked in formaldehyde for preservation," he warned us as he passed them out. "If you eat one, it will poison you. You have been warned."

Joey Ramirez sat back in his chair, looking disappointed, because Mr. Zammit had been talking mostly to him. Kenneth Lappin had dared him to eat part of the worm we dissected earlier this year. It was gross, and he'd gotten detention, but he'd also won five dollars, so he said it was worth it.

I glanced over at my lab partner, Aubrey Liu. She was new, and I didn't know her that well yet, so I wanted to see what she was thinking before I said anything. It was pretty easy to tell what she was thinking considering her face was all scrunched up like she'd bitten into an apple and found a spider nest inside. "Gross" she said as Mr. Zammit placed a cow eyeball on our lab table. It gleamed white and—surprisingly—blue against the table's dull black surface. "This is so disgusting," she moaned, then gagged.

I perked up. *Here comes Ruby for the win*. "Don't worry. I got this."

"You sound way too excited," she said, grimacing. I froze, worried I'd said something wrong, but then she smiled. "And I'm really glad for it."

I just smiled back. To be honest, I *was* really excited. Blood and stuff had never bothered me, and I was interested in how bodies and the world worked. Mr. Zammit said I'd be a great doctor when I grew up. "Or a serial killer," I told him.

I think he was actually a little scared before I told him I was kidding.

Anyway, I'd much rather have seen a pot full of eyeballs bouncing down the stairs. My family would probably still love me if I turned out to be a serial killer who collected people's eyeballs for fun and was careless enough to drop them, but dropping my grandma's famous matzah balls like this? The afternoon before she was supposed to serve them at the weekly Sisterhood meeting at the temple, the one she'd told me was extra important? They were going to *kill* me.

I winced as I heard footsteps coming toward the basement door. Maybe I could salvage this. If I could distract my grandma before she saw the mess, I could fix things.

The matzah balls had actually held together pretty well. Only a few had smashed apart. I could gather the other ones and give them a good rinse to get the basement dust off them, and nobody would ever have to know what happened.

"Don't come down here!" I called up to the half-closed door. The footsteps stopped, but my heart was still racing. "I'm . . . naked!"

"You're naked?" The voice sounded dubious. And it wasn't my grandma's. "Why . . . are you naked?"

I said a few words under my breath that would've gotten me grounded if I said them in front of my parents. It wasn't Grandma Yvette, but it *was* the only person whose voice I'd rather hear less than my grandma's. "Because I'm changing!"

"You are *not* changing in the basement." The footsteps started again. "What did you do, Ruby?" Not even giving me enough time to think up a better lie—rude!—the basement door swung open, revealing my cousin Sarah looking down at me from the top of the stairs.

It seemed like my cousin Sarah was *always* looking down at me. Both literally—like now—and figuratively because Grandma Yvette loved her more, and she knew it. Everybody knew it.

4

Which was why a simple thing like carrying this pot of matzah balls upstairs without spilling them was such a big deal.

Sarah sighed down at me. It even seemed like her sighs were gustier than other people's. Maybe it was an advantage of her being four months older than me. It didn't sound like that much—we were in the same grade and everything—but she'd had four whole extra months of breathing practice. "I can't believe you dropped them all," she said, then glanced over her shoulder. "What happened?"

"It wasn't my fault," I said. And it wasn't, really. Grandma Yvette had demanded I go get the matzah balls really quickly, so of course I took the stairs two at a time. But I knew Sarah wouldn't care, so my shoulders just sagged.

I knew better than to say anything about cow eyeballs and remind her about Mr. Zammit's class. Sarah and I had always had our classes together and had been lab partners last year when we dissected an owl pellet, but we'd been placed into different tracks this year. We didn't have *any* classes together for the first time ever. Whenever anyone brought that fact up, Sarah got all sad and slumpy, which was actually kind of funny compared to her usually perfect posture.

5

Me? I was usually slumpy. But it wasn't because Sarah and I were in different classes.

Sarah glanced over her shoulder again. Her shiny dark hair bounced as she did it, too, like it was trying to rub how shiny it was in my face. She always had it tied back in a ponytail, neat and never frizzy. Her blouses were always white, and they never had funny slogans or food stains on them. "Maybe we can—"

"What's going on?" Grandma Yvette's voice was a rumble that traveled all through the house, so hearing it didn't mean she was close. Maybe I could fix this before—

She appeared behind Sarah at the top of the stairs, wide enough to fill the entire doorway. Sarah was taller than me, but she seemed to shrink.

I had only a few seconds to speak. "I didn't mean to," I said hastily. "I'll pick them all up, I'll—"

Grandma Yvette's pale blue eyes bore down on me. I stopped talking immediately as she began, her voice quiet. A smile stretched out over her face, a big fake one that didn't warm her eyes even a little. "Ruby Diana Taylor, what in the world happened down there?"

That was one of her things. She liked to hear you admit to whatever wrongdoing you'd done. I had a lot of experience with this. "I dropped all the matzah balls," I

6

said, and then, quickly, "It was an accident. I'll pick them all up, and I'll—"

Her smile stretched wider. It was almost wider than I'd ever seen it. You'd think a wide smile would be good, but not always when it came to Grandma Yvette. "Unfortunately, I can't serve matzah balls that have been dropped on the floor to the Sisterhood."

I shrank under the force of that smile, under Grandma Yvette's smoke-yellowed teeth. It always kind of reminded me of the freeze face corpses sometimes got after death, pulling their lips back toward their ears, baring their teeth. "I can check the freezer to see if there's more," I said meekly. I knew there weren't any more. All the refrigerated matzah balls were rolling around on the floor, and there weren't any frozen ones, because I'd already checked. I just wanted to get out from under those pale blue eyes, icy enough to make me shiver.

Grandma Yvette shook her head. Her steel-gray bob didn't move. "What a shame, Ruby. What a shame," she said. She turned to Sarah. "My dear, it seems we'll have to make chicken noodle soup instead. Will you go down and fetch me some egg noodles from the pantry?"

I perked up. Maybe I could redeem myself. "I can get it!"

"No, Ruby." Grandma Yvette's voice was heavy. "You've

done quite enough today." She paused to let the weight of those words sink in. I slumped under them. "Clean the matzah balls up, and then you should get started on your homework before that *mother* of yours comes to get you."

The way she said *mother* made it sound like she was saying something like *hiveful of wasps* instead. Sometimes I thought Grandma Yvette would prefer having a hiveful of wasps as a daughter-in-law rather than my mom. Though then I would be half wasp, which would be both weird and cool. As long as I got the stinger or wings half and not the antennae half.

"Okay," I said, only it came out more like a squeak. It was enough, though, to make Grandma Yvette leave. She turned away and went back toward the kitchen, where the bubbling pot of chicken broth had probably over-flowed by now, just so that she could blame something else on me.

Sarah, though, came down the stairs. Toward me. I scowled at her for wanting to rub how much better at everything she was in my face, and then I remembered that Grandma Yvette had asked her to grab the noodles from the pantry. I moved to the side of the staircase so that she could get by without having to step on me.

But instead of going down to the pantry, Sarah knelt next to me and started scooping dusty matzah balls into her arms.

"You don't have to do that," I said. Why couldn't she just leave me to stew in my misery by myself?

She shrugged. "I don't mind." She cracked a smile. "I've missed you lately anyway. Now that we don't see each other in school."

Maybe I don't miss you, I wanted to say back, but I held my tongue. I didn't really want to spend more time than I had to in the cold, dark basement, so I just focused on getting as many matzah balls into the pot as I could. Even the ones that had rolled under the old furniture stored down here. If I forgot those, they'd grow mold and rot and attract mice, which I learned after the meatball debacle of fourth grade. Really, it was a miracle Grandma Yvette kept sending me to fetch stuff out of the basement fridge.

I got down on my knees and kneel-walked across the concrete floor. Grabbed a matzah ball from under the old high chair Grandma Yvette used to pull out when Henry was a baby (and probably when Sarah and I were babies, too). Snatched another one before it rolled under the leaning tower of boxes in the corner. I looked around as I tossed the balls into the pot. I didn't see any others—oh, there was one, trying to hide behind that treasure chest.

A treasure chest?

I crawled over eagerly, tucking the matzah ball into my pocket before focusing fully on the chest. It looked like one of those old-timey treasure chests you'd see in a pirate movie: shiny brown wood, flat on the bottom and curved on top. I ran my fingers over the surface, feeling the small carvings of grapes and palm trees. Funny how everything else was dusty down here, but this wasn't.

A bunch of years ago, when we were little kids—okay, maybe it was only a year and a half ago, when we were slightly littler kids than we are now—Sarah and I had a longstanding joke about Captain Brickhead, which had started after this one time we saw a fast-food mascot standing guard over a giant pile of bricks. All one of us had to do was say "Brickhead," and the other one would burst into laughter. For Sarah's eleventh birthday, I'd made her a treasure map that led her on a scavenger hunt for Captain Brickhead's hidden treasure (conveniently enough, his hidden treasure happened to be a stash of Sarah's favorite snacks and a few of mine, since Sarah's favorite snacks were mostly far too healthy for my taste).

But that was before the Incident. Before the lines were drawn.

I shook my head, bringing me back to reality. There was one big difference between this chest and a real pirate's treasure chest: It wasn't locked. Which meant I could open it and check out what was inside. My fingers eagerly found their way down to the latch and—

"Stop!"

I fell back at the sound of Sarah's shout, right onto my butt. I winced but made sure to wipe it clear off my face and put on an annoyed look before she could see it. She stood by the staircase, her hands on her hips, looking down at me.

Of course.

I frowned at her. "What?"

"The chest." She took a few steps toward me, but stopped far enough where I couldn't reach her if I'd tried.

I bet I could nail her with the matzah ball in my pocket, though. Not that I'd actually do it. But I could if I wanted to, assuming it hadn't gotten too squashed when I fell on my butt.

She went on. "I found that in the back of Grandma's closet two nights ago. I asked Grandma Yvette about it and she told me never to open it. And then she took it and put it down here."

"But why would she—" I stopped short and squinted at her. "Wait, what were you doing here two nights ago?" My parents and Sarah's parents, my aunt and uncle, had us come here on the bus after school a few days a week to spend time with each other—something we used to ask for—and help Grandma Yvette. It was better than being in daycare. But I hadn't slept over here since my parents went on vacation without me two years ago.

Sarah pursed her lips and looked down at her feet. "I was sleeping over."

"Is that the first time?"

She shrugged, looking back up. She bit her bottom lip, then sighed. "No."

Meaning she'd slept over here before. Maybe a lot. And she and Grandma Yvette had never said anything, because they didn't want me to know.

My cheeks got hot, but I ducked my head. I didn't want her to see. "Whatever."

"Well, here are the matzah balls." She stepped over and dropped a matzah ball back into the pot with a *plop*, drying her hands off on her shirt. "You should be more careful."

"Thanks," I said, and I hope she didn't miss the sarcasm. If she did, she didn't let on. She just gave me a tiny smile, then moved around me to go get the noodles. She took them upstairs to Grandma Yvette, leaving me alone in the cold and the dark.

CHAPTER TWO

THE KITCHEN UPSTAIRS WAS WARM and steamy with the smell of chicken soup. I dumped the dirty matzah balls in the garbage, then rinsed out the pot in the sink. I stepped up beside Grandma Yvette, who was stirring the soup on the stove. Maybe if I was quiet and even meek, she wouldn't remember she'd told me to go sit in the other room and do my homework. She'd forget she was mad at me and she'd give me that smile, that focus, that love, that made me feel like I was the center of the universe.

"Smells good," I said.

"Homework," she replied. Okay, so that didn't work. I took long steps out of the kitchen, pausing in front of the fridge. Photos of little me and little Sarah grinned back at me, along with my brother Henry, Sarah's brother Joseph, and various cousins. But the centerpiece of the fridge was a drawing Sarah had done of Grandma Yvette's dead dog, King. I hated to admit it, but it was pretty good. It looked almost like King was getting ready to lunge off the page and bite my ankles, his favorite activity when he was alive.

Then again, I reminded myself, King had basically been a mop of hair. So, Sarah's drawing hadn't really been *that* hard.

I sighed through my nose and continued into the living room, where I sank into the puffy red velvet couch. It enveloped me like it was trying to swallow me up.

I just had to be better. I knew why Grandma Yvette liked Sarah more than me, but I could change her mind if I stopped messing up all the time. If I could just be *better* and listen more and not do things like drop matzah balls down the stairs and . . . and . . . I don't know. There had to be a way. Because Grandma Yvette was my *grandma*. The only one I had, considering my other grandparents lived in Florida, which was basically the moon. I'd read and heard enough stories about grandparents to know that they were supposed to love you unconditionally, which means no matter what. So if your grandma, who spends a lot of time with you, *doesn't* love you unconditionally, doesn't that mean there's something wrong with you?

Grandma does not like Sarah more than you. She likes you both the same, echoed my dad's voice in my head. *There's nothing wrong with you.* But he wasn't here with us all the time. He hadn't heard what I heard during the Incident. He didn't see me messing up, like dropping everything and trying to open treasure chests.

I sat bolt upright. The thoughts I had about how I needed to be better scattered like I'd thrown a rock at a flock of birds. Which I would never do. "Grandma," I called into the kitchen. When she didn't respond right away, I hopped to my feet and peered in the doorway. She was rolling out some kind of dough on the counter while Sarah mixed up a bowl of what looked like raspberry jam. Probably making her famous raspberry thumbprint cookies.

I didn't have time to think about the cookies. Even if they were my favorite cookies in the world. I tore my eyes away from the jam and found the back of my grandma's steel-gray head. "Grandma?"

"What is it, Ruby?"

I watched her hands scrunch the dough, then pound

it out. Scrunch it up, then pound it out. "You know the chest downstairs? The one Sarah found in the closet two nights ago?"

Part of me hoped that Grandma Yvette would pound out the dough one last time and then turn to me, frowning, her head cocked. *What do you mean, two nights ago? Sarah never comes here at night. She must have been lying to you, Ruby, because I'd never have one of my beloved granddaughters sleep over and not the other.*

But she didn't even pause in her rolling out. "What about it?"

I felt myself deflate a tiny bit, like someone had pricked me with a pin. "Well," I said. Did I even care about this chest so much, or did I just care that Sarah had gotten to sleep over when I hadn't? "Why did . . ."

I trailed off. I couldn't say that. I could just picture Grandma Yvette's disappointed expression as she shook her head. *Don't be petty, Ruby. I know you can do better than that.*

I sighed. "The chest," I said again. "Sarah said we weren't supposed to open it. What's in it?"

This time, she stopped rolling out the dough, but it was so she could turn around and look at me with serious eyes. Like, gravely serious. Like she was about to tell me my dog had died. And even though I didn't have a dog, I was kind of nervous anyway. "You must never open that box," she said.

"But it's not even locked," I said. "If it's that important, why don't you lock it?"

"Because hitching a lock through the opening would mean opening the box a tiny crack." Her voice, husky and raspy from years of smoking gross cigarettes, lowered even further. "And the box must *never* be opened." She bent toward me, eyebrows knitting themselves together with what looked like anger, and—

"Grandma," Sarah interrupted. "The jelly is smooth."

Grandma Yvette didn't even turn to her. That's how serious this was. But she did straighten up, her eyebrows loosening a bit. "I mean it, Ruby. You can *never* open that box."

"But *why*?" Grandma shook her head at my question, but I pressed on. "Where did it come from? What's in it?"

She leaned forward. This close, I could smell the smoke that always clung to her hair and her clothes. "A *dybbuk*."

Sarah let out a little gasp, so I gasped, too, even though

I didn't know what a dybbuk was. Sarah said, "But dybbuks aren't real."

"Who are we to say what of Hashem's creation is real or not real? That's a job for the rabbis and scholars, not us," Grandma Yvette said. Sarah shrank a little bit under the words, and I had to fight not to look smug at *her* getting told off for once. "The box came with my grandparents from the old country when they fled."

I had only a hazy idea of what the old country actually was. I thought it was somewhere around Russia and Poland and Hungary, off in Eastern Europe where the winters were long and cold and the people hated the Jews. Fortunately for me, my great-great-grandparents had all escaped the old country before the Holocaust, when at least six million Jews—and lots of other people deemed "undesirable" by the Nazis—had been murdered.

Sometimes I let myself think about the fact that if I'd been there back then, I would have been killed just because of who I was. Who my family was. Plus Sarah, and my parents, and my dumb baby brother, and Grandma Yvette, and Aubrey—my (hopefully) new friend at school. It sends a shiver down my spine.

Grandma Yvette continued talking about the box.

"Before my grandparents died, they left the box to me and gave me a warning. Someone had used the box to trap a dybbuk, and now it was my duty to guard the box so that the dybbuk could not break free."

So what was a dybbuk? Some kind of monster? Another shiver raced down my spine, but this time it was a delighted one.

"But more important," Grandma Yvette said, "if you open the box, you won't just face the dybbuk." She fixed me with a piercing blue eye. It pinned me in place like a dead butterfly on a bulletin board (which I've done once, but only when I found the butterfly already dead). "You'll have to face *me*."

I stood frozen for what felt like a whole minute, until Sarah interrupted again. "The jelly is smooth."

Grandma Yvette turned back to Sarah, her smile growing over her face again. It was like a spell had been broken. "Great. We'll assemble the cookies."

That meant I was dismissed. I wandered back to the red velvet couch, but I didn't bow my head over my math notebook. Math could wait. Instead, I grabbed my phone and googled what a dybbuk was.

Trusty old Google directed me to the correct Wikipedia page, which I read with rapt attention. It told me that a dybbuk was a malicious possessing spirit from Jewish mythology that stayed on Earth to complete some goal, sometimes after being helped.

So basically, a dybbuk was an evil ghost who took over another person's body in order to achieve some earthly goal.

Cool. I kept on reading. Only a pious Jew could exorcise it—get rid of it. Great! There were lots of Jews around here.

But I couldn't open the box. Or Grandma Yvette would get mad. And I was already trying to be better for her. To be more like Sarah. If I opened that box and let out the dybbuk, she'd be furious. I'd never catch up to Sarah.

Even if I was, like, 99 percent sure dybbuks weren't real.

It was hard to focus on ratios and percentages when there was even a 1 percent chance that Grandma Yvette had an evil ghost trapped in her basement. And it became harder to focus when Sarah, carrying a few cookies in a napkin, came out to ask me if I needed help, and accidentally left them behind on the table (I had to eat them, of course). Fortunately, my homework wasn't all that hard, so I finished it before my mom came to get me.

I didn't waste a chance to broadcast that information. "I finished my homework," I said, popping into the kitchen. "So I can help more, if you need me."

Grandma Yvette turned to me from where she stood near the counter and graced me with a rare smile. Well, a rare *real* smile. "Thank you, Ruby. We're nearly finished, but you're such a dear."

I preened under the attention. The fact that they were almost done made it even better, because it meant I was getting credit for not doing anything. For one brief moment, I was on top of the world, good and worthy, important.

And then the doorbell rang. My mom was here. Grandma Yvette and I walked to the front door together, me stopping to grab my backpack on the way as she opened it. My mom smiled at Grandma. "Hi, Yvette."

The word I'd use to describe my mom would be *shiny*. Her hair was shiny gold. When she smiled wide, which was often, her teeth were shiny white. Her lips shined, too, pink or red or whatever other color she put on them that day. It was hard for me to think of her as "beautiful" or "pretty" or whatever my friends told me. She was my mom, after all.

The gold cross around my mom's neck was shiny, too. Grandma Yvette didn't look at it as she smiled back at my mom. "Hi, Margaret."

My mom cleared her throat. "Ruby, are you ready to go? Henry's asleep in the car."

"Oh. Yeah."

I went over and let Grandma Yvette kiss me on the forehead. Her lips were papery and dry. "Good night, Ruby." She raised her eyes up to my mom and smiled so that all of her teeth were on display, including the pointy ones. "Good seeing you, Margaret. Give Aaron my love."

"I will." Mom beamed back at Grandma Yvette. It felt almost as if they were having a contest to see which one of them could smile the hardest. "Great seeing you, too, Yvette."

Mom sighed as Grandma Yvette's door closed behind her. "Did you eat at Grandma's?"

I shook my head as I climbed into the car. "Mom, have you ever heard of a dybbuk?"

"A dybbuk?" She looked over her shoulder as she backed the car out of the driveway. I looked over my shoulder, too, but at Henry sleeping in his car seat in back. He looked so peaceful and cute like this. It made me want to poke him.

Though if I poked him and woke him up, Mom would be mad. And I'd rather face down a dybbuk than Mom when she was mad.

Mom continued, "It sounds vaguely familiar, but I can't say I know what it is. Is it something you learned about at school?"

I shook my head and stared out the window. "Never mind."

I *really* wanted to open that box.

CHAPTER THREE

I WAS STILL THINKING ABOUT the box on Thursday afternoon when Hebrew school rolled around. My mom dropped me off at the front door with a wave. I usually ran up the stairs and straight inside, because I was usually late, but today I paused. Someone was sitting on the stairs, her knees pulled up to her chest and a sheet of black hair covering her face.

Maybe this is the beginning of a horror movie, I thought, a thrill running through my chest. The girl would slowly stand up, all her bones cracking menacingly, and the hair curtain would part to reveal a skull with fire in her eyes . . .

Except that then she shook her hair out of her face and revealed herself to be just Aubrey Liu.

"Hey, lab partner," I said. I shifted my stack of Hebrew school books in my arms. She jumped like I'd surprised her, even though she was the one sitting like something out of a scary movie. "How come you're out here?"

She shrugged. "Just didn't feel like going inside yet."

I stood where I stood. She sat where she sat. And then, at the very same time, we said, "Want to go in?" We laughed at the same time, too. Something warm tickled inside my chest.

She stood up and said, "So have you had any nightmares about the cow eyeball yet? Because I have." I laughed again as we walked inside into the main hallway. "Last night I dreamed that it came alive when you tried to cut it open and it rolled off the lab table and bounced into the hallway."

"Sounds fun," I said. We passed by the lower-grade Hebrew school classes—Alef and Bet—whose own alefbets were hung all along the hallway. They had to learn the Hebrew alphabet before they could advance to learning all of the prayers and Hebrew words like we were doing. Hebrew school also involved learning culture and history and holidays and things like that, all in the afternoon after regular school two days a week. "But no, I haven't dreamed about the cow eyeball at all." I paused, holding my breath for a moment. Should I tell her what I was really thinking about? What if she thought I was weird?

She glanced over at me, eyes wide open with … interest? Maybe? *It's okay. Let her think I'm weird.* I already had one friend—well, cousin—I had to hide my weirdness from. If Aubrey was going to think I was weird for being me, I'd rather know that now. "I actually had a nightmare about this box I found in my grandma's basement," I said. "She told me I couldn't open it, that it had a dybbuk inside, which is like an evil ghost. So now of course I can't think about anything *but* opening it."

She grinned. Her teeth gleamed like tiny pearls. "Oh wow, it's like Pandora's box!"

"What's that?"

We started climbing the stairs. The older kids, like us, had class on the second floor. It's like the teachers were telling us that we were finally old and strong enough to make the journey.

Her eyes bugged out a little bit. "You've never heard of Pandora's box?" Before I could say anything back, she clapped a hand over her mouth. "Sorry. That was rude," she said, her voice muffled. "I just really like Greek mythology. My big sister spent years telling me those stories. I remember sitting in the bath and she'd tell me about Scylla and Charybdis and the sirens, all monsters that lived in or near the water. When I walked with her on our neighbor's farm to look at the cows, she told me about Argus, who was the son of a cow-nymph, and who was a giant covered with a hundred eyes . . ." She stopped short and finally took a breath. She tilted her head. "Mostly monsters, really. Maybe that's why I'm a little scared of her."

"You're scared of your sister?" I asked. "And no, I've never heard of Pandora's box." But I did really like how passionate she was about it. It reminded me of how I felt about the chest. Or cow eyeballs. "What is it?"

Aubrey stepped to the side of the hallway so that other kids could get by. Her sleek black hair brushed against a big mural of Adam and Eve in the Garden of Eden some long-ago class had painted. "My sister is eighteen. And she's a track star, and she's first chair on the flute, and she's, like, the most beautiful person ever. And there was a box, and this woman Pandora was told not to open it."

It took me a second to realize that Aubrey was talking about two different things. But the thing my mind stuck on most was the first thing: She had a sister who was just like Sarah! Well, maybe not just like Sarah, but she sounded perfect. Like Aubrey felt overshadowed. Like me.

It made me want to give her a hug.

But she was staring at me, like she was waiting for me to respond, not hug her. So I said, "But of course Pandora opened the box." It wouldn't be a very good story if she hadn't.

"Yup," Aubrey said. "And you know what was in the box?"

Sarah swished by me and touched me on the shoulder, angling her head toward the door of the classroom, her ponytail pointing the way. I knew what she wanted. For me to follow her in, the same way I did every day.

Except I didn't really want to right now. So I nodded back at her, then toward the door. *You go ahead without me. I want to hear the end of Aubrey's story.*

A surprised look crossed Sarah's face for a moment. She hovered by the door for another moment, as if waiting for me to join her. But when another couple of kids came up and couldn't get through because she was blocking the way, she swept into the classroom with them.

Okay. Back to Aubrey. What was in the box? "A vampire folded up like an accordion?"

Aubrey blinked. "What?"

"That was my dream," I said. "What was in there?"

"*All the evils of mankind,*" she exclaimed. She tossed her

hair. "If Pandora hadn't opened the box, we wouldn't have things like hunger, or illness, or *death*."

I pursed my lips. "So you're saying she shouldn't have opened the box."

She shrugged. "She probably shouldn't have." She smiled wide. "But that doesn't mean *you* shouldn't."

"Sit down, everybody!" Mrs. Rosen called from inside.

"We'd better go in," I said, and we walked in together.

The classroom was bright, both window-wise and color-wise, decorated with various pictures we'd had to draw over the course of the Hebrew school year. Sarah's, naturally, were front and center: her illustration of Noah's ark, all the animal pairs looking so lifelike I half expected to hear them roar or whinny; Moses parting the Red Sea so that the Israelites could flee Egypt, an expression of real fear on his face.

Sarah was sitting in the middle of the very front row, as usual. She gestured at the seat next to her, where I always sat.

But Aubrey was already winding her way through the desks, to her spot in the third-to-last row. She sat down and looked at me questioningly. There was an open spot beside her, too.

I looked from Sarah to Aubrey. Aubrey to Sarah.

Then stared all the way to the back of the room, where Kenneth Lappin was rolling around on the floor for some reason, and made my way to the seat next to Aubrey. I sat down without looking back at Sarah, like maybe Sarah would think I hadn't seen her. She couldn't be upset if I hadn't seen her.

I knew it wasn't true. But as I sat down in that comfortable middle seat, with rows of other kids protecting me from Mrs. Rosen's laser eyes, it still felt good. Safe. People would look at me, and they wouldn't see Sarah at the same time. That felt even better.

"You're sitting with me today!" Aubrey said. Or cheered. Quietly.

I stared down at my desk and slouched all the way back in my chair, like that might keep Sarah from seeing me. I kept my eyes on the back of her head. "I need a break from Little Miss Perfect."

It was funny, saying that out loud, considering for so long we'd begged our parents to let us spend all our time together. Once when we were little, I'd tried tying my wrist to Sarah's after a sleepover so that her parents couldn't take her home (it didn't work, because scissors existed). We'd just had so much fun together back then.

Aubrey said, "Yeah, I can't believe you're related."

I tensed. "What does that mean?"

"I didn't mean it like that," Aubrey said hastily, and I spared a glance up at her to see her face was scrunched up, too. Like she was worried she'd hurt my feelings. "I don't think she's perfect. She's just very prim and proper, and you're not."

Mrs. Rosen stepped up to the front of the room. She looked tired. She *always* looked tired. Probably because she had six kids. "*Shekket, bevakashah.*"

Quiet, please. As the buzz of words around me calmed, I leaned over to Aubrey and hissed in her ear. "She's not *just* prim and proper. She gets, like, a hundred percent on every test, and every grown-up loves her, and she knows exactly how to—"

"Ruby!" Mrs. Rosen snapped from the front of the room. I snapped back into my seat, my face heating up, and mentally added one more item to the list. *Sarah never gets yelled at for talking during class.*

Once we were all quiet and facing forward, Mrs. Rosen went on. "Class, we have a very special guest today."

She paused as if building suspense, but we all already knew who this *very special guest* would be. One of our two rabbis had died a month ago—of old age—and last I'd heard from Grandma Yvette, they were close to choosing a new one. That was actually what that matzah ball soup had been for—the Sisterhood was having a welcome dinner for the new rabbi.

It was pretty important, I guess, since the rabbis were the people in charge of our temple. And our spiritual growth, said Mrs. Rosen. But I didn't really care too much. They were just old men with long beards. The new rabbi would be another old man with a long beard.

I blinked back to the conversation to see Mrs. Rosen nodding at Sarah, who'd apparently answered a question while I'd been off in my head. "Right, Sarah," Mrs. Rosen said, smiling wide. "I'll be bringing the new rabbi in here for an introduction. I think you'll be very excited to meet Rabbi Ellen."

Rabbi Ellen? That was a strange name for an old man with a beard. In my experience, rabbis were named Harold or Melvin or Abe.

And then a woman walked through the door, a *kippah*—skullcap—worn on her short silver hair. I didn't usually see women wearing *kippahs*—during services married women generally covered their heads, but they usually wore little lace caps they picked up from a table at the front of the room.

Later, I felt stupid at how long it took me to put the

pieces together, but honest to Hashem, I didn't realize who the woman was until she said, "Hello, class! I'm Rabbi Ellen."

Rabbi Ellen?

I surveyed her in a new light. She was old, but not super old, like the last rabbi. Like, around grandma old. She was short and solid, built like she could withstand a hurricane, and had bright brown eyes that peered at us from a pale, round face. No beard in sight. Not even a little one.

"I understand that I'll be the first female rabbi ever in your congregation," she said. "Which is very exciting for me!" A few murmurs went around the room. I saw Ernesto Rojas nudge Max Wolfe in the shoulder and whisper something in his ear. I scowled at him, even though for all I knew he could've been affirming how exciting this all was. I felt very protective of Rabbi Ellen all of a sudden. I had no idea why, considering she'd spoken only four sentences in front of me and she didn't know my name, but I did. "Let me tell you a little bit about myself," she continued.

"I grew up in New York City, just an hour away. How many of you have been to New York City?"

Everybody raised their hands except for Talia Weissman,

who'd literally just moved here from Los Angeles. Rabbi Ellen gave us a brisk nod. "I worked as a teacher in a Jewish school for more than twenty years, and then I felt a calling to do something more, so I enrolled in rabbinical school. I loved that I'd still get to teach, but my class would be the entire congregation!"

She stopped and looked out at us. "Do any of you have questions for me?"

To nobody's surprise—or at least, not to mine—Sarah's hand shot up. Her arm made a perfectly straight line pointing up toward the ceiling. Rabbi Ellen nodded at her, and the arm fell back down to rest neatly on Sarah's lap. "My name is Sarah," she said.

"Hi, Sarah."

Hi, Sarah, I mimicked in my head, wrinkling up my face.

Sarah continued, "All of our rabbis before have been men. I've never met a female rabbi before. Do you feel like a trailblazer?"

She sounded like she was reading out of a textbook or something. I made another face at the back of her head.

"Sarah, that's a very good question," Rabbi Ellen said. *Ugh.* "The answer is yes. Some people aren't ready for such a change. Sometimes it's blatant and obvious, like the man who pulled me aside after services one day and told me that he believed women shouldn't be rabbis, and sometimes it's more subtle. Less obvious. For example, often when I'm attending an event with my husband, and when people hear that one of us is a rabbi, they immediately turn to him. Even though the number of female rabbis, especially in places like New York City, is growing quickly."

She smiled. I didn't know why, because what she was saying about the way she'd faced a lot of sexism didn't exactly make me want to smile. It made me want to punch Max Wolfe in the back of the head for snickering even as Mrs. Rosen gave him a warning glare. "But you know what else?" Rabbi Ellen continued. "I've experienced so many more positive things. Girls and women who are excited to have a female role model. People of all genders who are supportive and happy for me. I've met with many people in your congregation, and with very few exceptions, everybody is excited for me to get moving!"

She talked for another few minutes about our responsibilities as young Jews, blah blah blah, before finishing up. "I hope I'll get to talk to each of you individually over the next few months as I settle in," she said. "I'm especially excited to hear about your bar and bat mitzvah progress.

I know most of you have started working with the cantor on preparation already."

I had. Torah reading was hard. Sarah, of course, thought it was easy. I glared at the back of her head, then furrowed my brows. I sat just enough to the side of her where I could see a sliver of her face, and it was hard to glare at someone wearing an expression like that. She was gazing at Rabbi Ellen with . . . I don't know, something like love. Her whole face was glowing. Not literally, of course, that would be creepy. But it was like there was a light shining behind her eyes.

Her hand shot up again before Rabbi Ellen could leave. "Rabbi Ellen? I have another question for you," she said, which was unnecessary. "I talked to Mrs. Rosen a while back about starting a junior chapter of the Sisterhood, but she said I should wait and talk to you because she was busy." Mrs. Rosen's eyes narrowed at Sarah, like she wanted to pinch her but she never would because she was an adult. "Could we do that?"

Rabbi Ellen smiled wide and nodded. "Mrs. Rosen spoke with me about that, too! I'd love to start a junior chapter of the Sisterhood."

Starting a club was one of Sarah's favorite things to do. She'd started no fewer than seven clubs when we were little kids, ranging from the S&R Club (which only allowed members whose first names started with *S* or *R*) to the Detective Club (where we'd solved crimes like "who stole the TV remote and hid it," which turned out to be me in an effort to give her a crime to solve). In six of them we were the only members. By the seventh, my brother Henry was big enough for us to enlist him as treasurer. Three-year-olds are terrible with numbers, as it turns out. But I was always an excellent vice president, which was easy, since vice presidents typically don't do much.

Sarah's hand shot up again, then faltered. Rabbi Ellen nodded at her, then she lowered it. "Nothing," said Sarah. Her voice was very quiet.

"Well, Junior Sisterhood sounds wonderful," said Rabbi Ellen, and Sarah let out a *whoosh* that sounded like relief. "Would you please circulate a sign-up sheet for other girls?"

"Of course!" said Sarah. Her head whipped around, and her eyes settled on me, burning fiercely into my forehead. "I know Ruby wants to join!"

"You do?" I squeaked. I squirmed in my seat. I swore I could see smoke drifting up from my burning skin. It felt kind of like guilt. I'd left Sarah all alone in the front of the room. So I don't know if it was that or the fact that I had always been her vice president or the resolve in Sarah's eyes that made me say, "Right, I do."

Next to me, Aubrey shifted in her seat. I peered hopefully in her direction. Maybe I could salvage this and turn it from what sounded like "being forced to cook in temple" to "being forced to cook where at least I had a new friend." "Aubrey, maybe you want to sign up, too?"

She shrugged. "Sure, why not?"

Rabbi Ellen clapped her hands together. "Wonderful. I'll reach out to your parents and work on setting up a schedule." She smiled at us one more time, then left. Once the door closed behind her, Sarah's eyes dimmed to their normal look, aka serious and boring. Mrs. Rosen stepped back to the front of the room and clapped her hands.

"I'm glad we all got a chance to meet Rabbi Ellen!" she said. "Now, let me hand out last week's quizzes. We had one perfect score—*mazel tov*, Sarah!"

I spent most of the rest of Hebrew school doodling Grandma Yvette's creepy dybbuk box in my notebook. Class came to an end all too slowly. Aubrey had to wave me a quick goodbye so that she could run out to meet her sister, who was picking her up. Sarah caught up with me as I walked down the hallway at a more leisurely pace. "Hi, Ruby," she said, sounding out of breath, like she'd run to catch me or something.

"Hi, Sarah. Congratulations on your perfect score." I hadn't gotten *that* far below a perfect score. A ninety-three was still an A. But tell that to Grandma Yvette. I only got a hug and that smile that made me feel like the center of the world when I got a ninety-five or above.

"Thanks," she said, still breathless. A few strands of hair had come loose from her bun and now drifted around her face. It made her look a little . . . softer, somehow. Which made all my muscles clench up. Was she going to confront me about picking a different seat?

Of course not. Sarah would never cause a scene. "Thanks for agreeing to join Junior Sisterhood," she said. "I made sure to put you on the sheet."

"Oh great," I said. "Thanks." *Thaaaaanks.* There was no way I could back out of it now.

"Don't mention it," she said. "Anyway, I wanted to talk to you because Grandma's supposed to take me out for ice cream to celebrate my last report card."

Something dark stirred in my chest. *This* was why she'd run to catch up with me? So she could rub it in my face?

She was only perfect when the grown-ups were around. I was *glad* I'd ditched her to sit with Aubrey.

She kept talking, but I couldn't hear any of her words through the sound of my own heart beating in my ears. My fists balled at my sides. If I didn't get out of here right now, I might say something I'd regret. Or punch someone I'd regret.

"My mom's waiting outside," I said loudly, stopping Sarah right in the middle of whatever she was saying. Her mouth widened into a perfect little *o*. "Have fun with Grandma."

I sped up and hopped into my mom's car. As we drove away, I could see Sarah standing on the front stoop of the temple, her hands tucked into her coat, her shoulders hunched against the cold.

CHAPTER FOUR

I DON'T REMEMBER WHEN I first realized that Grandma Yvette liked Sarah more than me. I just remember being maybe four or five and asking my dad. *Don't say things like that,* I remember his voice rumbling. *She loves you both the same.* When I asked my mom the same question, she said, *Let's talk about it more later. For now, eat your peas.*

We never got to later, somehow.

I do remember when I learned why. The Incident. I'd auditioned some other names for it—the Great Fissure, the Big Break—but none of them stuck quite as well.

It happened less than a year ago, but somehow it felt so much longer. Maybe because it was kind of a dividing line for me. Between the innocence of being a kid to the . . . what was the opposite of innocence? Guilt? But I didn't have anything to be guilty for. At least, I didn't think so.

It started off as just a regular day: me and Sarah at Grandma Yvette's, helping her cook for some event. She hadn't worked before Grandpa Joel died, but ever since he'd passed away, she'd "needed someone to cook for." So now she catered kosher meals for family and friends, mostly through the temple. We helped her roast some salmon with dill, red onion, and capers on top and then boiled some rice and steamed some green beans with lemon before my dad got there to pick me up.

So maybe it hadn't totally been a regular day, considering my dad never really picked me up from Grandma Yvette's. He was a lawyer and that meant he usually didn't get home from his law firm until right before dinnertime, sometimes not even till after. But today my mom had something going on, so here he was. I ran to open the door for him, since Grandma Yvette was busy with the salmon. "Hi, Mom!" he shouted, poking his head in the door.

"Hi, dear!" Grandma shouted back, but she didn't come out. Which was kind of weird, because a few nights before when Uncle Ezra showed up first to pick up Sarah, she ran out of the kitchen to say hi and left me in charge of continuously stirring the risotto to make sure it didn't scorch (it didn't, which earned me the biggest, glowiest smile and warmest hug when she got back into the kitchen).

Dad turned to me. He was still in his suit for work. "Ready to go?"

"Ready to go, Mr. Penguin," I said, because the suit was black and white and made him look a little like my favorite Antarctic bird. He laughed as we walked out together, me telling him about how school had been and him telling me how work had been (just as boring as school, it seemed).

I stopped short just before I got in the car. "Wait! My math book." I'd taken it out of my backpack and put it on the table, hoping at some point I'd feel like doing my math homework, but of course I hadn't. It was still there, waiting for me.

"Go run and get it."

I did. The door was unlocked, so I opened it and slipped inside. *There.* I grabbed my math book off the table and tucked it under my arm, turning to go.

". . . about Ruby?"

I stopped short at the sound of my name drifting from the kitchen. In Sarah's voice.

Why was Sarah talking about me behind my back? That very back was now stiffened with surprise.

"What *about* Ruby?" Grandma Yvette said. Moving very slowly, like they might hear my footsteps, I pressed my back up against the wall to hide. "She doesn't need to know the rules of a kosher kitchen."

Sarah was quiet for a moment. "Maybe not. I know she doesn't keep kosher, but it might be good for her, too."

I bristled a little bit at the idea of Sarah thinking that something was "good for me." What was she, a grown-up?

"My dear," said Grandma Yvette, and now her voice was hard, a tone I didn't hear a lot from her when she was talking to Sarah. "Judaism says that in order for someone to be Jewish, either they must be born to a Jewish mother or they need to go through the conversion process."

She didn't say anything else, but my heart was beating so hard I thought I might throw it up. Obviously, she was talking about me. And she didn't have to come out and say what she meant: *Ruby's not Jewish the way we are.*

My mom was Catholic, just like her parents and my aunts and uncles on that side. Traditionally the Jewish religion is matrilineal, which means it's passed down from mother to child. So for most of Jewish history, if your mom wasn't Jewish, *you* weren't Jewish. Even if you celebrated all the holidays and knew all the prayers and everything.

Things are different now. At least in my temple they are. There, I'm considered Jewish even though my mom isn't Jewish. They call me a patrilineal Jew. But patrilineal Jews like me aren't accepted as part of the religion everywhere. Like in other, more traditional synagogues, for example.

Sarah's mom is Jewish, of course. So nobody could ever tell *her* she's not part of the people. That thought made me bristle again.

Grandma Yvette gave a little laugh. "Besides, you know Ruby. Such a dear, but she'd spill something or dump flour all over the floor or blurt out something silly, and then we'd never get to the point."

I waited for Sarah to stand up for me. The way I would as her perpetual vice president. To tell Grandma Yvette what she surely believed, even if I'd never heard her actually say it. *Grandma, Ruby is just as Jewish as we are. The temple says so and everything.*

And yet she didn't. She just said, very quietly, "What's the first step?"

I bit my tongue so that I wouldn't start shouting. How could she betray me like this? What else had she said behind my back? Did she really not think of me as Jewish like her?

I didn't want to ask her, because I didn't want to talk to her at all. Everything in my head was clicking together. How Grandma Yvette had always preferred Sarah to me. How she could do no wrong. Her smug manner when she spoke to me, because she knew my attempts to be better would be useless. Nothing could change your blood.

Grandma Yvette's front door eased open again. My dad poked his head in. He opened his mouth to call my name . . . and then closed it when he saw me frantically shaking my head, my eyes bugging out. That movement freed me up enough to scuttle toward the door. "What was that?" I heard Grandma Yvette saying as it closed behind us.

"What's going on?" Dad asked me once we were safely in the car, maybe because I was taking deep breath after deep breath—in through my nose, out through my mouth—in an effort not to cry.

Now I knew why Grandma Yvette liked Sarah more. And even worse, Sarah knew, too, and she didn't care. But what came out was, "I wouldn't spill anything. I'd be really careful."

"What do you mean?" Dad said, turning to look over his shoulder as he backed out of the driveway.

He wouldn't get it. Nobody could ever tell him he wasn't Jewish enough. "Never mind," I said, heaving a sigh.

He glanced at me sidelong. "Did your grandmother say something to you? Because she—"

"No," I said, and didn't even feel bad about it, because she hadn't said anything *to me*. She'd said it behind my back. "Hey, what's for dinner?"

I didn't care about what was for dinner. I didn't even remember what it was, only that it tasted like cardboard. All I cared about was that now I knew that something was wrong with me, and I'd never be able to forget it.

Even though I knew I should just let it go, I couldn't stop thinking about the dybbuk box. If I'd seen that box in her basement on a normal day, I probably wouldn't have given it that much thought. There were a *lot* of boxes in that basement. But to be told I *couldn't* open it because there was an evil ghost inside?

As soon as I got to Grandma Yvette's house the next week, I dropped my backpack on the floor with a *thud*. Sarah, who'd probably placed her bag gently onto the ground, winced at the loud noise. "Did you hear about the new rabbi?" I asked. Before Grandma could answer, I went on. "It's a woman. Rabbi Ellen."

Grandma Yvette's lips pinched together. "Yes, I've heard."

Right. She was part of the temple's old-person squad. They knew everything. "Do you like her?" I asked. I didn't want to volunteer my opinion before knowing how she felt.

Sarah chimed in before Grandma Yvette could. "*I* really like her. Grandma, did you hear about how we're starting a Junior Sisterhood chapter?"

"That's wonderful, darling," Grandma Yvette said. "I'm happy to help if you have any questions about planning dinners and organizing parties." She smiled big. "You're so good at cooking, I'm sure you'll be a natural Sisterhood leader. Just like Joseph was a natural at studying Torah."

Sarah's shoulders slumped a bit, her arms going limp at her sides. I thought about defending her and saying that Sarah was a natural at studying Torah, too, except that I didn't exactly want to defend someone who'd roped me into Junior Sisterhood. I'd tried to back out of it when I got home, but my parents had already heard, and they were so thrilled about me taking an "interest" and being "excited" about "extracurriculars" that they wouldn't let me.

And Grandma Yvette had never answered my question. "But what about Rabbi Ellen? Do you like her?"

Grandma Yvette took a moment to answer, looking thoughtful. "She's a lovely woman. But just that: a woman. Who's taking care of her family while she's on the bima?"

I scowled, feeling weirdly defensive over Rabbi Ellen. "I don't know, maybe her husband?"

Grandma Yvette shook her head. "I don't know, it just doesn't sit right with me. We have traditions for a reason."

Traditions? Like, traditions that meant women couldn't do certain things? Things like studying Torah and Jewish law? Okay, now I was getting kind of annoyed. "Is that why Joseph never had to cook with us?" Joseph, Sarah's older brother, used to come over to Grandma Yvette's house with us, too, only he never had to assist in the kitchen. He'd hang out in the living room and play on his phone as he pretended to do homework. Sometimes Grandma Yvette had Sarah and me make him snacks. "That's not fair!" I glanced over at Sarah to back me up, but she was staring at the floor. Wasn't Sarah just as annoyed as I was?

"Joseph's not here, and he was always so diligent at studying I would've hated to tear him away from his books," Grandma Yvette said. Her big giant smile was back, even though she was basically saying, *I am happy to tear you two away from your books, though.* Which would have been fine by me, if not for the reasoning behind it.

But I knew what she wanted to hear, and since Sarah clearly wasn't going to chime in, that meant there was room for me, even if I had protested already. I straightened my back. "You're right, traditions are important," I said, which was true, even if I wasn't specifying which traditions I thought were important. "Without tradition, we wouldn't have any of our holidays or anything. And I love our holidays." Well, the holidays except for Yom Kippur, which was a fasting day, because not eating for an entire day made me really cranky. "So I guess I agree."

And there it was: *the smile.* Not the big fake smile. It softened into something real, something glowing, something entirely focused on me. It made me feel like I was the center of the universe. No, it made me feel like one of the two things at the center of the universe, and for once, this thing that was me sat atop the other thing that was Sarah.

Grandma Yvette said, "I'm glad to hear that, my dear. Now, if you could go downstairs and get me some raisins for the kugel?"

I snuck another glance at Sarah. Still staring at the floor. Sarah was always diligent about her books, way more diligent than Joseph, but if she wasn't going to speak up for herself, I wasn't going to stick my neck out even farther for her. Especially not while I was on top. But now was my chance to investigate the dybbuk box, so I left that queasy feeling behind me as I went to the basement.

Usually I didn't close the basement door behind me when I went downstairs because it cut off my escape route in case there were monsters or something hiding down there, but today I did, even with the possibility of a real monster lurking. I neared the dybbuk box, using my phone as a flashlight to really get a good look at all of its details.

It was super old, definitely. Weathered with age, almost something that I'd see in a museum. The carvings on the sides were worn halfway to smoothness, and the brass hinges were a burnished green. It even smelled old, but the whole basement kind of smelled old.

My fingers drifted toward the opening. All they would

have to do was flick upward just a tiny bit, and it would be—

"Ruby!" Grandma's voice cut through the closed door like it was nothing but air. "I need those raisins, dear!"

I leapt to my feet like the box had shocked me. "Coming!" I hollered up the stairs.

I was halfway up by the time I realized I'd never gotten the raisins.

Evil ghosts didn't actually exist, so what could be in that box?

Grandma Yvette had never looked inside. But that box had come over from the old country with her grandparents, meaning that her grandparents may have been the ones to put stuff inside and tell their own child—my great-grandmother, Ruska, who I'd been named after—not to look at it. There could be treasure inside.

Or maybe not treasure as in *treasure* treasure, as in gold bars or diamonds, but treasure to Grandma Yvette and our family. She talked a lot about how so much Jewish history had been lost because of the Holocaust. What if there was Jewish history here, undiscovered and ready to be examined?

I bet that would make Grandma Yvette so happy. Happier than Sarah could ever make her.

And it would be *my* history, too. Maybe it would remind her about that. Make her realize that I'm just as Jewish as she is.

Grandma Yvette was currently occupied with mixing up the kugel, with Sarah at her side. Sarah had been really quiet today, which was nice. I didn't have to hear about every single thing she was being successful at. All that made it easy for me to slip out of the kitchen and downstairs to the ground floor. If they asked where I was going, I had a story planned out. *I'm just going to the bathroom. Seems like it's going to be messy, so I might be a while.*

But neither of them asked. They just let me go.

I hesitated in front of the basement door, glancing off to the side. There was a little den down here on the ground floor, one that opened out into the backyard. I used to spend lots of time down here when I was a little kid, playing with the plastic trucks and army men and puzzle games in the box of toys that was Henry's now.

Gus lived in the den, too. Right now he sat in the fake leather armchair, the one that stuck to the skin of my arms and legs on hot days. I liked the *thuck* noise it made when I peeled my skin off it. Gus's arms and legs were bare as he smiled at me from beneath his dark mustache, but his limbs wouldn't stick to the chair no matter how hot it got.

That's because Gus was made of cloth. But he was more than a *doll*. He was almost life-size—bigger than me, at least—and Grandma Yvette always dressed him in some of Grandpa Joel's old clothes. Today he was wearing a Rutgers University T-shirt and basketball shorts.

The weirdest thing about Gus? You know how most dolls are just smooth plastic or bare cloth under their clothes? Well, not Gus. Gus was what Grandma Yvette delicately called *anatomically correct*. Meaning he had real private parts and everything under there. Apparently Grandpa Joel had bought him for her years ago as a prank, and he'd stuck around. Sarah and I used to pull down his pants and giggle at his bare butt when we were younger and less mature.

"Sorry about all that, by the way," I told Gus. He just smiled back. That was the good thing about Gus. No matter what I did or what I said, he smiled at everybody the same way.

Enough of Gus. I was just trying to distract myself. I took a deep breath, pulled the basement door open, and launched myself down the stairs.

The box was waiting for me. As I expected—it wasn't like it was going to pick itself up and go running off. Grandma Yvette could have moved it, I guess. Really, why *didn't* she move it? If she really thought it was dangerous, you'd think she'd hide it away. So maybe she really did want someone to open it and just wasn't brave enough to do it herself.

I flexed my fingers. Something in my wrist cracked. Okay, I was stretched and limber. Time to do it. Time to go.

I crouched down and reached toward the box. I extended my fingers and touched the wood and—

"What are you doing?"

At least this time, I didn't jump at the sound of Sarah's voice and go falling backward onto my butt. Instead, I just pressed my lips together. I didn't even look back at her. "I didn't hear you come down."

"You're not supposed to touch that, Ruby," she said. "You're going to get in trouble."

Her voice was quiet and unassuming, just as it had been during the Incident I didn't like to think about and yet somehow couldn't *stop* thinking about. Something inside me just . . . snapped. Like a Popsicle stick underfoot.

I leapt up and turned to face her. Her hair was in a

slicked-back ponytail like always, not a strand out of place. Her clothes were neat and tidy. Somehow she'd even managed to walk down the stairs all quiet and lady-like, not "clomping like an elephant," as Grandma Yvette had once said about me.

I opened my mouth wide, like I was going to yell, but what actually came out was quiet. "I am *so sick* of hearing you talk."

I hadn't even touched her, but she jerked back like I'd slapped her. "What?"

I went on. "I am so sick of *you*. Of how *perfect* you are all the time." I mimicked her voice. "*You're not supposed to touch that, Ruby. You're going to get in trouble.*"

Her face had gone shock white. "I don't sound like that."

Of course she'd be worried about how she sounded, rather than anything else I'd said. It made me want to spit fire. "I'm *always* being compared to you, you know that?" I said. "And I'm *always* coming up short. That's why Grandma Yvette likes you more than me. I'm *so sick* of it, and I'm *so sick* of *you*. Why do you think I ditched you at Hebrew school? Because I got a taste at school of what it's like *not* sitting next to you all the time, and it was really, *really* great."

The silence that followed after I spit that last word was deafening. Her whole face had pinched up. Her shoulders were rigid. The cords in her neck stuck out like ropes she wanted me to grab. She finally said, "Why are you being so mean?" Her lower lip actually trembled. "I *miss* you. I feel like I barely get to see you anymore."

"Well, I don't miss *you*," I spat back. All my muscles were clenched. "Hanging out with Aubrey is so nice. So relaxing." I shook my head, then went in for the kill. "Just because we're cousins doesn't mean we have to be *friends*."

All the air went out of me at once, and I deflated. I hadn't realized how heavy those words had been, and how much I'd hurt carrying them around all the time.

Sarah still just stood there, frozen. And then her face pinched up. "It's not *my* fault you're not as good as me." Her words felt like a punch to the stomach. And she was looking even angrier. What if she actually hit me? She might surprise me and—

She took a big step toward me.

Maybe she *was* going to hit me! I jumped back to avoid any flying fists . . .

. . . and fell right over the dybbuk box.

Sarah shrieked. I fell backward onto some cardboard boxes that knocked the wind out of me, but kept me from breaking my head on the concrete floor.

When I got back to my feet, I realized the box was open.

CHAPTER FIVE

SARAH SCRAMBLED BACKWARD TOWARD THE staircase—away from the open dybbuk box. I leaned over it, a dark, guilty thrill going through me, and peered inside.

There were three things in it. A small paper card, crumbling with age, covered in words written in Hebrew letters—maybe Yiddish. A scrap of red fabric. And a white handkerchief, yellowed in places, with a splotch of a rusty-brown stain in the middle.

"Is that blood?" I mused, squinting at it. I wanted to pick it up and look at it more closely, but there was an air of the sacred around the contents of the box. Like touching it would have been disturbing a grave. Which I would have done, but only if there was a good reason, like how in the old days doctors used to raid graveyards for bodies to dissect for learning purposes.

Sarah didn't respond, so I looked up. She was standing there like a statue, her mouth back in that perfect little *o*. I felt a rustle of annoyance . . . and hurt, after what she'd said to me. She was probably thinking about how she was going to race upstairs and tell on me, since I wasn't as *good* as her. "It was an accident," I said. "I only tripped over it and opened it because *you* were going to hit me." I didn't really know if she was going to hit me, but that seemed like better leverage than *I only tripped over it because you took a step toward me and I panicked.*

She still didn't say anything, so I reached out and pushed the box's lid. It snapped shut. What a disappointment.

"Well, I'm going upstairs," I said. That should have prompted some kind of response, even if it was for her to move out of the way, but it didn't. She just stared at me, wide-eyed.

I didn't know what to do. I couldn't just *leave* her here. I was maybe, kind of, a little, beginning to feel bad for what I'd said to her. It was all true, but I definitely could have said it in a nicer way.

That didn't mean I was going to apologize, though. Because she'd been mean back to me. I reached for her hand and gave it a small tug. "You're freezing," I said with some surprise. It felt like she'd just pulled her hand out of the refrigerator.

"Girls?" Grandma Yvette's voice floated down from above.

That stirred Sarah from her stupor. "We should go upstairs," she said. She sounded oddly formal and emotionless, like she was holding back everything she actually wanted to say to me.

"Let's go upstairs," I said. I could pretend with the best of them, too.

Grandma Yvette was waiting at the top of the stairs. "What were you two doing down there?"

"Nothing," I said, then held my breath. It was up to Sarah now. She could get me in trouble, or let me go.

"Nothing," Sarah echoed.

"Good," Grandma Yvette said. "Sarah, your dad is here to pick you up. He's in the car outside."

"Okay," said Sarah. She drifted toward the front door. Grandma Yvette had to chase her down to give her a kiss on the forehead.

I hung back. I knew what Mom would say about my

argument with Sarah. *You can't avoid hard topics. You have to talk about them, or else they'll just fester inside you and make everything worse.* I couldn't pretend I hadn't said those things to Sarah forever.

But I *could* do it for one night.

CHAPTER SIX

WE GOT OUR SCIENCE TESTS back the next morning in class. I'd gotten a 103 percent on my cow eyeball diagram. Aubrey had gotten an eighty-eight. "I should've paid more attention," she moaned. "It was just so disgusting."

Mr. Zammit had written "disturbingly lifelike!" on mine. The extra three points were for coloring it all in with my four-color pen. I smiled down at it. Grandma Yvette would hang it on her fridge.

I tucked it away in my folder as Mr. Zammit returned to the front of the room. He clapped his hands together. "Now that we've finished up with our cow eyeballs, it's time to move on to our next unit."

I didn't bother raising my hand before asking my question. "Do we get to dissect something else?"

"The next unit will not involve a dissection," Mr. Zammit said. My arm slumped down and hit my desk. "We will be continuing on in our study of anatomy, however, with a look at the brain."

"Can't we dissect a brain?"

"Unfortunately, we are not allowed to dissect human brains in sixth-grade science," he said. "Unless you would like to volunteer yours?"

I shook my head, and I swore just then I could feel my brain sloshing around inside my skull. "Right, I didn't think so," Mr. Zammit said. "Luckily for all of you, I have this great PowerPoint. Feast your eyes on my excellent special effects!"

"Oooh!" said the girl in front of me. I rolled my eyes at her, safe knowing she couldn't see me. Jamilah was a little bit of a know-it-all; she raised her hand at practically every question Mr. Zammit asked, even once she'd already answered a question or two and knocked off her participation credit for the day. Sometimes, when Mr. Zammit told her, "Great job!" Jamilah's black braids all shook with excitement. Thank goodness for Aubrey being in my class or I might have gotten stuck being lab partners with her. She was like Sarah 2.0.

A few of the kids in the front groaned as Mr. Zammit opened up his title page, but I sat up straight in my seat. Not for Mr. Zammit's special effects (by "excellent special effects" he meant that he'd figured out how to add music and graphics to the PowerPoint slides, which any third grader could do). I'd really liked digging into the worm and the cow eye. Not because I was some kind of psychopath who liked blood and guts, but because I really liked seeing how things worked inside. The cow eye was apparently pretty similar to a human eye, and now every time I looked at something, I pictured the light reflecting through the cornea (bluish gray) and the lens and the vitreous and focusing in on the retina, which processed them into electricity and sent them through the round, stiff optic nerve.

But the brain. That was even cooler than the cow eye, even if I didn't get to cut one open. I wanted to see how people thought. What made them feel certain things. Maybe if I learned how things like that worked, I could make—

BRRRRIIIIIIING!!!

I jumped in my seat, knocking my knees hard on the underside of my desk. But that hurt less than my head, since I sat right under the fire alarm, which was currently screaming like I was personally on fire. In front of me, Jamilah was clutching the sides of her head, trying to cover her ears.

Mr. Zammit's thick black eyebrows knitted themselves together. "Huh. There was no drill on the schedule," he said, and then shrugged. "Okay, class. Line up!"

"If it's not on the schedule, does it mean it's a real fire?" hollered Joey Ramirez. He definitely didn't have to shout *that* loud to be heard over the fire alarm.

I popped out of my seat. "If it's a real fire, we should probably jump out the window. Just to be safe."

"We *are* on the first floor, so we'll all probably be fine," Aubrey chimed in. I grinned at her. She grinned back.

"If we make it out to the door and it's entirely blocked by flames, I promise that then you can jump out the window," Mr. Zammit said solemnly. "Until then, I need you to get in your lines."

Even though taking the time to get into neat, orderly lines and file quietly into the hallway would probably get us all killed (or at least horribly burned) if there was a real fire, we did so anyway. The air outside was crisp and cool, and of course I'd left my coat behind in my locker. I shivered, rubbing my arms.

Aubrey said, "Wimp," but she grinned at me, so I knew she was kidding. She wasn't shivering at all, even though she was only wearing a T-shirt. One of those freakish people who never got cold.

Unlike me. I jumped from foot to foot, trying to warm myself up. It made me think of how I'd jumped yesterday, when I'd stumbled over the box. I took a deep breath. "Can I ask you advice?" I asked. Aubrey had told me about her perfect older sister. Maybe she'd be able to help me with Sarah.

"I love giving advice," Aubrey said brightly. "Shoot."

Before shooting, I glanced around to make sure Sarah wasn't within earshot. She had language arts right now, which was on the other side of the building, but you never know. "You know my cousin, Sarah? So we got into a big fight last night."

"You did?" Aubrey regarded me with solemn eyes. "What happened?"

I took a deep breath. "Well, you know the dybbuk box I told you about?" She nodded, and I recounted what had happened in the basement last night, every little dirty detail. "So I feel kind of bad, but I don't really want to apologize, either, because it was all true," I finished, then waited for Aubrey's wisdom.

And waited.

And waited. Aubrey chewed on the inside of her cheek. "Don't get mad," she said eventually. "But I think you should apologize. Yeah, she was kind of mean, but she only said that because you were mean first."

I sighed, then jumped up and down a little more, then crossed my arms tightly over my chest, trying to keep the warmth in. The dead brown grass of the athletic fields crunched under my feet. "I was afraid you'd say that," I told her.

"Sorry," she said. "But you know, she's your cousin. And you obviously hurt her feelings. So even if everything you said was true, I think you should still apologize for how you said it. Maybe you can sit down with her and tell her you're sorry for yelling at her, but you do feel frustrated sometimes because she always seems to be doing better than you."

I thought about saying those exact words to Sarah and wrinkled my nose. Part of me knew Aubrey was right . . . but the other part of me felt like telling Sarah that would be like slicing my dissection scalpel down my chest, cracking open my ribs, and letting Sarah roll my heart around in her hands.

"I don't know," I said.

"It worked when something like this happened between me and my sister," Aubrey said. "It was a year or two ago and I was really bugging Clare, like making a lot of noise on purpose while she was trying to practice her flute, and she yelled at me to stop being the worst sister ever." Her lips turned down at the memory. "So I yelled back at her that *she* was the worst sister ever, but I didn't really think so, it was just because she'd hurt my feelings. It sounds like kind of the same thing."

"I don't know," I said again. "She hurt my feelings first." And I told her about the Incident, which made me feel a little sick by the time I was done. And yet when it was all out and on Aubrey's shoulders, I felt somehow a little better. Like how throwing up doesn't feel good while it's happening, but your stomach usually feels better when it's over.

"I don't know if I'm getting out of that what you are," said Aubrey. "Like, it doesn't sound like Sarah was on your Grandma's side to me."

Of course she'd agreed with Grandma Yvette! Before I could reply, I felt a tap on my shoulder. Aubrey looked over, and her eyes widened, so I knew who it was before even having to turn around.

"Hi, Sarah," I said, and she stepped over in front of me. She was totally bundled up in her fluffy coat, the faux-fur lining of the hood covering half of her face. Her hands were shoved deep in her pockets. The parts of her cheeks I could see were bright and rosy. "Did you hear what we were talking about?"

She shook her head, her eyes wide. "Should I have?"

"It doesn't matter," I lied. "What are you doing over here? Isn't your class all the way on the other side of the building?"

"I was carrying a message to the principal's office. My language arts teacher always asks me to do it."

"Right," I said. "Anyway..." Aubrey raised her eyebrows at me, then lowered them, then raised them again, her eyes practically bulging out of her head. I could almost hear her trying to communicate with her mind. *Do it now, Ruby, apologize to your cousin!* Subtle, she was not. "Anyway, I..."

Heavy footsteps trod nearby, and two of the vice principals stopped in front of us. "Hi, girls," one of them said. "Please show us your hands."

I pulled my hands out of my armpits and held them

up. Aubrey, however, glowered at them suspiciously. "Why?"

"Because the fire alarm was pulled. There's no fire, so we believe someone did it as a prank," said the vice principal. Not a very funny prank. Why couldn't this prankster have chosen a warm, sunny day? Not that there were very many warm, sunny days in early December. "The fire alarm squirts a purple ink stain on the hands of anyone who pulls it that's very hard to wash off."

"We were in class with Mr. Zammit when the alarm went off," said Aubrey, but she still held her clean, pink hands up in front of her. "See?"

The vice principal nodded, then turned to Sarah. This time when he spoke, he sounded almost apologetic. "I know you had nothing to do with it, Sarah, but—"

"I know you have to see everybody's hands. It's fine!" She pulled her hands out of her pockets and waved them quickly in the air. Unsurprisingly, they were totally clean. She shoved them back into her pockets before they could freeze.

"Thanks, girls." The vice principal nodded at us again, then they both moved on to the next cluster of kids.

Aubrey rolled her eyes. "No way it was a girl who did it," she said. "He should be looking at all the boys. Only boys are stupid enough to pull a fire alarm on a cold day like this."

"That would be discriminatory, though," Sarah said. "They could probably get sued."

Aubrey shrugged. She didn't look too bothered about it.

"Anyway, did I see you taking a picture of the poster for the spring musical?" Sarah continued. "With the tryout information?"

Aubrey's face flushed. "I didn't realize anyone saw me."

Sarah gave her a tiny smile. "Sometimes people tell me I would make a great spy."

Most of Sarah's smiles were tiny smiles, come to think of it. Had I ever actually seen her cheeks break in a wide, spontaneous smile that showed all her teeth?

I butted in. Sarah wasn't going to steal Aubrey from me, too. "Are you thinking about trying out?"

Aubrey gave a shrug even tinier than Sarah's smile. "I don't know. I'm new. And I'm just a sixth grader. I don't know anyone, and I probably wouldn't even get in, right?"

"You can't say that," I said. "What play are they doing this year?"

"*Beauty and the Beast*," Sarah said. "And Ruby's right. Sixth graders are usually cast in the chorus, but sometimes if they're really good, they get a main role."

Aubrey gave another tiny shrug. "I have to think about it. I'm also really nervous about singing in front of people."

"I'll help you rehearse," I told her.

"Thank you!" she said, her whole face shining, and then the bell trilled.

"Let's go, people!" Mr. Zammit called. "Back inside! If we hurry, we can still watch my PowerPoint!"

"Lucky you," Sarah said. She had Mr. Zammit earlier in the day. "He learned how to animate the text so that it bounces all over the screen. Good luck taking notes."

Well, the joke was on her, because I wasn't planning on taking any notes.

"Gee, thanks," Aubrey said dryly, then went to line up. I started to follow her, but Sarah grabbed me by the arm.

"What is it?" I asked.

"I need you to do me a favor." Sarah's face had gone entirely serious. The tiny smile was gone.

"What is it?" I asked again.

At this point, I had exactly zero suspicions. I thought maybe that she wanted me to take extra notes from Mr. Zammit's PowerPoint since the animated text had bamboozled her so much this morning, or that she wanted me to encourage Aubrey a little more so that she felt confident enough to try out for Belle.

Sarah was always so good that I didn't even get suspicious when she darted her eyes to the sides, like she was making sure no one was looking at her as she hunched over to pull something out of her pocket. All I could see was a handful of knitted cloth before she shoved it into my hands.

"Hold onto these for me, okay?" she asked. "Please?"

I went to unfold the cloth, but she laid her bare, cold hands atop mine to stop me. "Just take it." She lifted her hands. "I'll come back for them later. Just don't let anyone see them. I'd better get back." Without a goodbye, she turned and hurried away, not even giving me a wave over her shoulder.

Weird.

I turned my attention to the knitted cloth. It was . . . unpleasantly damp. I unfolded it, and my jaw dropped open.

A glove. It was one of Sarah's winter gloves, the knitted green ones her non–Grandma Yvette grandma had made for her last winter.

And it was covered in a purple ink stain.

CHAPTER SEVEN

"RUBY?" AUBREY CALLED. SHE WAS already in line behind Mr. Zammit. "What are you doing?"

My heart beat quick and fast like a rabbit's as I stared at Sarah's purple ink–stained glove. I couldn't believe what I was seeing, because what I was seeing was impossible, because it suggested that Sarah was the one who'd pulled the fire alarm, and I knew *that* was impossible. So there had to be some other explanation.

It was probably something sickeningly good. Like she'd pulled the alarm to stop a bully from dumping another kid in a trash can, and was waiting for the fuss to die down before reporting it. Or someone had grabbed her glove and used it to pull the alarm, but she didn't want to tell on them because she'd rather talk them through their feelings, which would make this person realize that they had to come clean on their own to become a better person.

Because the Sarah I knew would *never* pull a fire alarm. Not just because it would interrupt the school day and all the learning she needed to make sure she did well in middle school so that she could do well in high school so that she could get into a top college. But because she'd get punished, hard. Like, police hard. Suspension—or even expulsion—hard. Hundreds of dollars in fines hard.

And what reason could Sarah possibly have for pulling a fire alarm? She liked her language arts class. They were reading *The Diary of Anne Frank* right now, which was one of Sarah's favorite books. She had it practically memorized and looked to Anne as an example of a "shining light." They even looked kind of alike.

I shook my head. I'd talk to Sarah later and get her explanation, which would most likely make me nauseous with how good and true and selfless she was. Until then, I had a PowerPoint to watch.

But Hebrew school didn't give me any chances to get Sarah alone. First of all, it was slow getting in because of the security guards out front (apparently there'd been some kind of threat against Jewish organizations in the area), which meant I had to bolt to make it to class on time. We did a full run-through of the Saturday morning service, then practiced some Chanukah songs for the upcoming holiday. All the while, Sarah managed to be on the opposite side of the room from me.

When we only had fifteen minutes left, Mrs. Rosen gathered us in our classroom. "I thought it would be nice if we all wrote letters of welcome to Rabbi Ellen," she said. The tone in her voice said that it didn't matter if we thought it would be nice or not, we were all going to be writing letters of welcome to Rabbi Ellen. "They don't have to be long, but I want everybody to tell her they're happy to have her here."

I heard Ernesto Rojas whispering behind me. "You know what I'm going to write? 'I'm happy to have you here.' Exactly that."

Max Wolfe snickered. "Me too."

I rolled my eyes. Stupid boys. I pulled out a pencil for me and a pencil for Aubrey—I'd noticed she'd chewed hers in half—before leaning down over my paper. Then leaning back up.

Up in front, Sarah was bent over her own paper, her elbow shaking as she scribbled furiously away. I wondered what she was writing. Probably something beautiful and eloquent Rabbi Ellen would read aloud to the whole congregation so that everybody could gush over what a talented writer and sweet person Sarah was.

"Five minutes!" Mrs. Rosen announced.

"Crap," I muttered under my breath. I'd been so busy thinking about Sarah that I hadn't even started my own letter yet. And I wasn't going to be like the boys and write one stupid sentence. I might not be Sarah, but I had *some* standards.

Dear Rabbi Ellen. That was easy.

Welcome to Congregation Ahavat Olam! I bet I'd get some extra points for spelling our temple name correctly. *We are all really happy that you're here to be our rabbi.* Basically the same as the boys, but taken up a notch. *I think it's really exciting that you're going to be the first female rabbi at our temple. I've never had a female rabbi before and I think it's really inspiring.*

Boom. Who doesn't like to hear they're inspiring? I finished it up with a flourish: *Sincerely, Ruby D. Taylor.* Adding a middle initial always made your name look more professional.

"All right, class, finish up whatever sentence you're writing and hand your papers forward," Mrs. Rosen announced.

Double-boom, finishing just in the nick of time. I passed my paper to the front. Sarah was still writing, writing, writing. Seriously, we'd met Rabbi Ellen *one time*—how much could she possibly have to say?

The bell rang to end class, and I got up, ready to confront Sarah. But she was still writing. And just as I turned to Aubrey to ask her what she wrote, Sarah jumped up, slammed her paper down on Mrs. Rosen's desk, and raced out the door. "Wait!" I called after her, but she didn't stop. I went to follow, though I knew I'd probably get yelled at for running in the hall, but Aubrey stopped me.

"She must be really excited about our first Junior Sisterhood meeting," she said as she gathered her books.

Ugh! I'd forgotten our first meeting was today. Now I wasn't going to get any of my homework done tonight. Though, to be fair, I probably hadn't been going to do my homework tonight anyway. That was what the bus ride to school was for. So what if it made my handwriting a little shaky? It was like Mr. Zammit's fancy PowerPoint effects, but on paper. (He did not see it that way.)

"That makes sense," I said. Aubrey and I walked out together, down the stairs into the main hallway, where we had to push our way through a crowd of little kids milling about. "Where are we going? The social hall?"

The social hall was the all-purpose room of the synagogue: sometimes a party space, sometimes used for
overflow seating when a major holiday fills up the sanctuary. I'd won two goldfish there during Purim carnivals
and also eaten whitefish salad there for lunch following
Shabbat services. I apologized to my goldfish when I got
home, but they didn't seem especially bothered by my eating their cousins. (To be fair, I probably wouldn't have
been bothered if a giant goldfish had eaten Sarah.)

Speaking of Sarah, she was not in the social hall. Rabbi
Ellen was in the process of dragging a small round table
from the edge of the room over the nubbly green carpet
into the middle; Aubrey and I rushed to help her by dragging some folding chairs from where they rested against
the pink striped wallpaper. We surrounded the table with
chairs, then looked around. "Where's everybody else?"

Rabbi Ellen smiled at us, but it was the same kind of
smile I gave the doctor after she asked me if the shot had
hurt so that she wouldn't think I was a baby. "This first
meeting is only you two and Sarah, it seems," she said. She
must have seen my face fall, because she added hastily,
"I'm sure more girls will join once we share the news with
all the other classes."

Or nobody will join because Sarah was the only person

who would possibly want *more* Hebrew school. I wanted to sigh and put my head down on the table, but also I didn't want to make Rabbi Ellen feel bad that nobody wanted to join her club. "Where is Sarah?" I asked, glancing around like Sarah might have been hiding under one of the tables. If she'd gone to the bathroom after Hebrew school or stopped to refill her water bottle at the fountain, she should be here by now.

"Let's give her a few minutes," said Rabbi Ellen. "In the meantime, we can get started with an activity I thought we might do."

She reached down beside her and deposited a big plastic bag onto the table. Out spilled a rainbow of old crayons, stubby and worn from their time in the primary classes. "I was thinking that since Chanukah is coming up, we might turn these old crayons into candles," she said.

That sounded like a craft for little kids. And there were a *lot* of crayons there, too. This was going to take forever with just a few of us. Sarah had better show up soon.

We gave her a few minutes. Then a few more. I texted Sarah and got no response. "She must have forgotten," Rabbi Ellen said after a bit. "We'll just start without her, then, and catch her up next time." A few crayons rolled across the table and plinked to the floor. Aubrey ducked down to pick them back up. "We'll start by taking all the wrappers off the crayons."

I started peeling with great reluctance, seething inside my head at Sarah. How dare she? The only reason I was here in the first place instead of sprawled out on the couch watching TV or reading a book or tormenting Henry was because she'd volunteered me. And now I was stuck here while she went off doing who-knows-what.

This time I did sigh and put my head down on the table, on top of a pillow of crayons. There was a reason crayons were not typically used as pillows: They're extremely uncomfortable to rest your head on, as it turned out.

"I get the feeling that you're not thrilled to be here," Rabbi Ellen said in my direction. "Why don't we talk about why?"

I lifted my head to see that Aubrey had already peeled a mountain of crayons, which made me feel guilty for not helping on top of everything else. I picked one up and dug my fingernails into a trusty old pink Razzmatazz. Should I be honest? Why not? What's the worst that would happen? "It's not that I don't want to be here," I said, even though it was. "It's just that I'm not very good at the things Sisterhood does. Like cooking. Or cleaning up. Or organizing parties. Or crafting." I gestured at all the crayons, even though I was kind of proving myself wrong, considering how much paper I'd peeled off already.

Rabbi Ellen smiled. "Well, we don't *have* to focus on that. This is a space for you. We can stop the candlemaking if you want." Her smile faltered a little. "I just thought it would be fun."

Well, now I felt bad. I shook my head and took to peeling extra hard to make up for it. "This craft is fine."

Her smile returned. "We can do what you want to do, and if you don't want to cook or craft, we can . . . hmm, learn more about Jewish law or history?"

"I like to cook," Aubrey said. She kicked her feet as she spoke. "My dad owns a restaurant, and he taught me and my sister how to cook from when we were really young. I think it would be fun to cook for the people here. And do, like, bake sales and stuff." Her swinging foot hit one of the metal table legs, making more crayons go rolling off the table. She stopped kicking. "Sorry."

"It's okay," Rabbi Ellen said. "Maybe we can do a little bit of cooking and a little bit of other things. I know Sarah mentioned to me that she was interested in some extra Torah study?"

"She did?" I blurted. She'd never mentioned that to me. I'd just assumed Sarah would want to cook and clean and set up events, the way she always did with Grandma Yvette. After all, she was "so good" at it. "But I thought Sisterhood was supposed to be focused on cooking and fundraising and all that? Isn't Junior Sisterhood supposed to be . . . well, a junior version of all that?"

Rabbi Ellen shook her head, a little smile on her lips. "Not at all."

"But my grandma says cooking for the congregation is an important Sisterhood tradition," I told Rabbi Ellen. "And don't we have traditions for a reason?"

"Traditions are great if the people want them and are happy with them," Rabbi Ellen said. "Otherwise they're just peer pressure from our ancestors."

I couldn't help laughing. Aubrey giggled, too.

Rabbi Ellen went on. "All my life, as far back as I can remember, my mother made these mandelbrot cookies with chopped apricots and dates in them for every holiday dinner. They were dry as dust to the point where my grandfather actually choked on them one year." She smiled at the memory. I assumed he hadn't choked to death, because she probably wouldn't be smiling. "When she stopped hosting and turned the responsibilities over to me and my siblings, she handed over the recipe for the mandelbrot cookies, too. I didn't make them for my first

Chanukah, and she didn't ask where they were. I think she was a little relieved not to see them on the table.

"So sometimes traditions are like that, where we do something over and over and we don't know why, because they're not very good," Rabbi Ellen said. "Sometimes traditions are like a plush, sweet honey cake, where everybody is happy to see it on the table every year. And sometimes they're like chocolate-covered matzah. Maybe some people really like it and want it on their tables for every holiday, and some other people don't like it and never want to see it again, and some people might be interested in having it for some holidays, but not all the time."

Okay, all this dessert talk was making me hungry. For one, I loved chocolate-covered matzah.

"So that's a long way to say that Junior Sisterhood can be whatever you want it to be," Rabbi Ellen said. "Within reason."

It was interesting how she'd spoken pretty much the opposite of what Grandma Yvette had said, even though they were both Jewish women around the same age.

"All right," Rabbi Ellen said. "Now we get to do the best part: smash the crayons into little pieces!"

That was indeed the best part. Aubrey and I shoved all the naked crayons back into their plastic bag, tied it up, and then took turns jumping up and down on them. The way they cracked under my feet made me feel like I was jumping on a bag full of cut-off fingers. Maybe even Sarah's cut-off fingers. "That's probably enough," Rabbi Ellen said, but I stomped a few more times for good measure.

When we put the bag of crushed crayons on the table, Rabbi Ellen had somehow come up with a couple of muffin tins. I looked at them warily, thinking she was going to spring cooking on us after all, but she explained that now we'd sort the crushed-up crayons into the tins. "I'll bake them later and put in the wicks," Rabbi Ellen said. "And voilà, candles!"

So we took to sorting. I divided my crayons by color and made a rainbow of different candles: one red, one blue, one green, and one kind of muddy brown where I shoved all the leftovers. Aubrey made some beautiful rainbow swirls.

It really was too bad Sarah wasn't here. She'd actually love this; she'd always loved drawing and art and stuff. Her candles would probably be the most beautiful ones of all.

As we sorted, Rabbi Ellen talked about some of the blessings. I knew pretty much all of the standard blessings, the ones we sang over wine (or grape juice for me) or bread or Chanukah candles, but as it turned out, there are about a million other ones, too. Ones to say when you see a rainbow or heard thunder or when you had a confusing dream. Even one to sing when you meet an especially wise person.

Aubrey closed her mouth around the last word and smiled, like it tasted good. "I'm going to sing this one when we go to science tomorrow and see Mr. Zammit," she said. "He'll think I'm casting a spell on him or something, but it'll really be a compliment."

"You should!" I said emphatically. The emphasis was because her voice was clear and strong and beautiful. "And you should really try out for the spring musical. You'd definitely at least get in the chorus."

Aubrey pursed her lips. "I don't know. I'm still nervous about singing in front of people."

"Are we not people?" asked Rabbi Ellen.

I cracked a smile. "Is there a blessing to sing if we find out we're not?"

All three of us laughed. Aubrey was still grinning by the time the laughs faded. "Maybe I'll try out. I'll think about it."

Maybe I wouldn't hate Junior Sisterhood. I'd think about it.

CHAPTER EIGHT

GRANDMA YVETTE WASN'T FEELING WELL, so I didn't see Sarah again until Hebrew school on Thursday. Mrs. Rosen was even slower going through the temple security than we were, which left my whole class to hang out in the hallway. Sarah stood by herself in front, closest to the door, maybe so that she could be the first one through. I went right up to her and stood, my feet firmly planted on the ground. She wasn't getting through me without a fight. At least not without giving me some answers. "So," I said.

"So," she echoed. "Did you hear that the local hospital is starting a shadowing program?"

I perked up. "Really?"

"Yeah, for middle schoolers. My mom was talking to Mrs. Kaplan, who's friends with Dr. Greenberg, who works there," she said. "She came to me to ask if I'd want to take part in it next year, but I told them they should talk to you instead."

I was so touched by this I didn't even know what to say back. "Like, any doctor? I could shadow someone in the emergency room?" That sounded extra cool because you could see how people were put back together after terrible accidents. "Ooh, or any kind of surgery, really."

"I don't know," Sarah said. "Dr. Greenberg is in the cancer part of the hospital, I think. But I can get more info."

The cancer part? The thought of that made me kind of queasy. I'd spent too much time in the cancer part of the hospital when I was eight, after Grandpa Joel was diagnosed with pancreatic cancer. The pancreas was one of those organs you never really thought about *until* it got cancer. The (unfunny) joke of it was that cancer in your pancreas was actually more vicious than cancer in most other parts of your body. Grandpa Joel hadn't even survived three months after his diagnosis.

"Thanks," I said, and smiled at her. Her telling me about this shadowing program reminded me of the time when we were ten and I'd tipped her off to a program I'd heard about at the town library, where a real professional artist came in to work with any interested kids. I did it with her so she didn't have to do it alone, and we'd drawn cartoon versions of each other. Like that time, she was being so nice. I'd almost forgotten why I'd—

Wait. No way was I some bird who could be distracted from its goal with shiny objects. Okay, maybe I was, but only a little. I leaned in close so that I could whisper right into Sarah's face and nobody else could overhear. "Why did you ditch me at Junior Sisterhood? You never answered any of my texts." That wasn't even the only thing! "And the glove! Did you pull the fire alarm?"

She stepped back. Which was wise on her part, because I spit a little when I whisper. "Yes," she said. I assumed that was in response to the fire alarm part.

I blinked. I'd expected her to deny it, or at least bandy about more, so I wasn't sure how to respond to such a blunt admission of guilt. "Why?" I finally said.

"Sarah?" Mrs. Rosen called from behind me. I turned around to find her at the door to the classroom, peering down at Sarah. She wasn't looking at her the way that teachers usually looked at Sarah: aka full of pride and warmth. The same way Grandma Yvette always looked at

Sarah. The way she occasionally looked at me, leaving me craving more.

Mrs. Rosen's lips were pursed, her eyes were narrowed. Her eyebrows were furrowed. She looked . . . confused. "I need to speak with you for a moment. In private." She was clutching a piece of paper between her hands so hard that it was crumpling a little.

I strangled a gasp. Did this mean Mrs. Rosen knew about the fire alarm? Was that paper a warrant for Sarah's arrest? Were they going to march her out of here in handcuffs?

"Ruby, are you all right?" Mrs. Rosen was looking at me strangely.

"Fine!" I said, but my voice came out about two octaves too high. Behind Mrs. Rosen, I noticed Aubrey squinting strangely at me, too.

Mrs. Rosen turned her attention back to Sarah, nodding at her. "Come with me."

Sarah nodded, her hands clasped before her, and followed Mrs. Rosen into our classroom. The door closed behind her so hard that the paper decorations of the animals that went on Noah's ark shook and rustled. One of the giraffes drifted to the floor. I leaned down to pick it up and pressed it up against the door . . . with my ear.

". . . shocked and very . . ." Mrs. Rosen's voice was fuzzy through the door, but that didn't disguise how stern those three words were. Like steel innocently covered by a fuzzy blanket—it would still stub your toe just as hard if you hit it. ". . . some kind of prank? If . . . not very funny . . ."

A poke on my shoulder. "What are you doing?" asked Aubrey. I raised a finger to my mouth and pointed at the door.

Mrs. Rosen was still speaking, and her voice was louder now. ". . . so rude and . . . uncharacteristic of you, Sarah . . . going to have . . . call your parents . . ."

I reeled back from the door, clapping a hand over my mouth. Was Sarah getting in trouble? *Was* it the fire alarm thing after all? But if it was the fire alarm thing, wouldn't Mrs. Rosen be calling the school and the police, not just my aunt and uncle? We'd learned in an assembly when we first started middle school about a twelve-year-old girl who'd pulled a fire alarm for fun and gotten charged with a felony, the most serious category of crime. She probably went to jail. Could she have gotten in trouble for missing Junior Sisterhood? Where had she gone then, anyway? Had her parents picked her up, not realizing that the meeting was that afternoon?

But now Sarah was talking. "Not me . . . don't know . . . who could have . . . I didn't . . ."

"What's going on?" Aubrey whispered.

I shrugged. "I don't know."

After a few minutes of indistinguishable hissing coming from behind the door, Mrs. Rosen opened it. I nearly fell over. "Come in, everybody," she said, her words clipped as she poked her head out into the hall. Sarah was already sitting at her desk in the front of the room. After what I'd heard, I expected her head to be bowed, for her to look sad, worried, contrite.

But it wasn't, and she didn't. Her head was held high, and there was a close-lipped smile on her face stretching from ear to ear. I tried to catch her eye and ask her a silent question, but she only stared straight ahead.

I followed her gaze. A slightly crumpled piece of paper sat on Mrs. Rosen's desk. I darted my eyes toward the door, where Mrs. Rosen was still ushering in the stragglers in the hallway.

Before I could formulate a good reason for or against it, my hand darted out and snatched the paper, then tucked it under my shirt.

"What are you *doing*?" whispered Aubrey behind me. I just gave her a warning shake of my head. Mrs. Rosen was within earshot. I didn't want her to know what I'd done. Not yet, anyway. Later on I could always put it back and apologize that I accidentally grabbed it thinking it was mine, or that it must have fallen onto the floor, because that's where I picked it up, thinking it was garbage.

I pulled it out right as I sat down, just in case Mrs. Rosen saw it was missing and asked about it right away. I wasn't going to lie to a teacher. Not straight-out like that. There was a difference between a bald-faced lie and a massage of the truth. At least *I* thought so.

"What is that?" Aubrey asked again, but I ignored her as I smoothed the paper out in my lap. It made a crunching noise, which I pretended was loud enough that I couldn't hear her. We'd both know that wasn't true, though. Which made me feel bad. I'd apologize later, but this was such a big deal I had to do it now.

Somehow it was way easier to think about apologizing for something little like this than something big like what I'd said to Sarah. Was that why Sarah had never talked to me about what Grandma Yvette had said about me? Because it felt too big and too scary?

Mrs. Rosen was saying something about how we had to divide up the verses of *Ashrei* for when we did our class Shabbat service, but my eyes were already on the paper in my lap. They snagged on the *Dear Rabbi Ellen* and *Sincerely, Sarah* at the end. So this was Sarah's letter to Rabbi Ellen. Maybe she'd been so floral in her descriptors of love and admiration that she'd made Rabbi Ellen vomit, and that was why—

I gasped.

> Dear Rabbi Ellen,
>
> You should go back to wherever you came from. We don't want you or your stupid junior sisterhood club hear. You smell bad and you look ugly. You dirty piece of crap!
>
> Sincerely,
> Sarah

I honestly didn't know whether to be more shocked by the words she wrote or the fact that she'd used the wrong "here" in the second sentence. They were both so un-Sarah that it might as well have been Haras ("Sarah" spelled backward). But this *was* her handwriting, even if it was messier than usual. It was easy for me to tell, because she had a very elegant way of curling the ends of her letters which teachers always thought was the prettiest thing ever.

"Hey, Ruby, my phone . . ." Aubrey whispered. I barely heard her over the thoughts whirling in my head. I certainly couldn't turn to look at her or I might start screeching them out uncontrollably.

How could Sarah have written this? Especially considering that she was the one who wanted to start Junior Sisterhood, not Rabbi Ellen? I wondered if she'd been able to convince Mrs. Rosen it hadn't been her. Maybe—adults tended to see what they wanted to see. And I was pretty sure Mrs. Rosen would want to see her perfect Sarah continuing to be perfect.

I spent the rest of Hebrew school staring at the back of Sarah's head, but it didn't give me any answers.

CHAPTER NINE

THE NEXT DAY, AUBREY GAVE me big, liquid puppy-dog eyes when I tried to say hi. She muttered a quick "hi" in response and turned to stare at the board, squinting at Mr. Zammit's daily do-now. *What is the largest of the three parts of the human brain?*

"It's the cerebrum," I said.

"I know," she said sadly.

Had her grandmother died from a stroke of the cerebrum or something? "Hey, is everything okay?"

She looked down at her desk. "I don't know. You tell me. You were ignoring me yesterday at Hebrew school. I didn't know if you were mad at me or something."

I let out a long breath. "Of course I'm not mad at you!"

She sucked that long breath in. "Are you sure? Because I was trying to tell you about how Clare made a joke in our family group chat about how everybody in our family sang like a dying cat, and my parents just sent laughing emojis and cat emojis like they'd forgotten I even existed."

Oof. I felt that. My whole life with Sarah, everybody had acted like she was so shiny with all of her achievements and perfect grades, while I was so dull no light ever reflected off me. If none of my pictures were hung up on the fridge, did I even exist? "You should show them how wrong they are," I said. "Now you definitely have to try out for the play." She didn't look convinced, but then I thought of something even better. "And hey, if Clare really does sing like a dying cat, this is something you can do that will set you apart. That will show her."

Aubrey's eyes widened like she hadn't thought about it that way. "Maybe . . ." she said. "So if you weren't mad, why were you being so weird yesterday?"

I hesitated. I still didn't know Aubrey super well, but if I blew her off again or made something up, I might never get the chance to know her super well.

And I wanted to.

"It's kind of a wild story," I said. "I don't know if you'll even believe it."

"Try me."

Mr. Zammit called for us to quiet down. He's kind of a stickler about phones, in that if he sees you even glance at yours during class, he'll confiscate it and keep it till the end of the day. Even if it's an urgent text, like the time Iris Joyner sent me advance knowledge that we'd be getting a pop quiz in history in last period. So I scribbled away in my notebook like I was taking notes on Mr. Zammit's very cheesy PowerPoint when really I was spilling all about the fire alarm and Sarah's letter to Aubrey. As he turned around to fiddle with the projector, I tossed the folded note—two pages long—over to Aubrey's desk.

With the way her face expanded and contracted at every twist and turn, it was hard for me to believe Mr. Zammit really thought Aubrey was reacting to his teaching. When she finished with the note, she folded it up and stuck it in her bag, then turned to me, her eyes almost popping out of her head. *Whaaaaaat*, she mouthed at me.

I know, right? I mouthed back, trying to make my eyes as wide as hers to emphasize just how shocking of a deal this was. *What do I do?*

"Ruby, Aubrey, do you have something you'd like to tell the class?" Mr. Zammit was staring at us from the front of the room, arms folded. Jamilah turned around in front of me and stared at me, too. I blinked in surprise—over her shoulder I could see that, instead of taking notes as I would have expected her to be doing, she'd been doodling a surprisingly accurate rendition of the human brain that appeared to be tap-dancing to an orchestra full of instruments being played by other human brains.

Mr. Zammit cleared his throat, waiting for a response. "No," Aubrey and I said together.

But we regrouped after class at my locker in the precious seven minutes we had to make it to our next classes, which, fortunately for us, were in the same wing and only a thirty-second shove down the crowded hallway. "What is going on?" Aubrey said breathlessly. "Are you sure it was her who wrote it?"

I really hoped I could trust Aubrey—I didn't think I could deal with all this on my own. "It was her handwriting," I said. "And she had to have pulled the fire alarm."

"Let me see the glove."

I looked around before taking it out of my locker, where I'd stored it since Sarah gave it to me to hide. It was the only place to keep it safe from Henry's sticky little fingers. Even if I didn't love that it was on school property, where the principal could technically stick his own fingers in it at any time. Sometimes they brought in dogs to do drug-sniffing searches, but I didn't think the dog would get excited about an ink-covered glove. Sarah had never asked for it back. Was it safe to throw it away at this point? But what if I needed it to prove to somebody that Sarah'd pulled the alarm?

"Here." I shoved it into Aubrey's hands. "Don't let anyone see."

She hunched over and opened the bunch of cloth, turning it over and over as she squinted at it. "It might not be purple ink," she said, but she sounded dubious.

"It's pretty obvious what it is," I said. "The question is why."

But we had no answer to that. We just stood there and stared at the glove until the warning bell chimed. I grabbed the glove and shoved it back into my locker, underneath the layers of books. "I'm not supposed to go to Grandma Yvette's for a few days, so I won't get Sarah alone for a while," I said. "And it's not really something I want to ask over the phone, you know?"

"I know," Aubrey said. "But there's got to be some explanation."

I thought about it all the way through history and the bus ride home. When I leapt off those high steps and landed on the pavement in front of my house, my mom was waiting for me, clutching tight to Henry's hand.

I tousled his hair. "Hey, Hen." He beamed up at me. He usually hated when people tousled his hair like that, but he actually liked when I did it. Not to brag or anything, but Mom and Dad said he "worshipped" me. Like I was some kind of goddess, or at least a big-time celebrity.

And I'm not going to lie, I loved it.

I looked up at Mom. She looked shiny, as always, but maybe a little tarnished today. Like someone had forgotten to polish her. "What's up?" She almost never met me outside at the bus stop anymore. It was right in front of our house, and she'd told me, *Ruby, you are almost a teenager and you are perfectly capable of walking up to the house on your own.*

Mom opened up her mouth, but before she could say anything, the phone rang. My mom sighed as she dragged Henry inside to get it. The house phone, which nobody ever used except... "Hi, Mom," my own mom said. I closed the front door behind me. Sometimes it was weird to think about my mom having a mom, too. That one day long ago she'd been my age, talking to her mom the way I talked to her now.

I called my grandma on Mom's side—my mom's mom—Nana, and my grandpa was Poppy. They lived most of the year in Florida, but came up every year at Christmastime to stay with my mom's sister. Nana always carried caramels in her pocket that crinkled whenever she moved, and Poppy liked to yell at the TV—not just at sports shows and news shows, but even if what was on was a cooking show or a kids' cartoon.

Like Grandma Yvette, Nana and Poppy hadn't been thrilled that their daughter was marrying someone of a different religion than them. My cousin Joseph—Sarah's older brother—told me a story once about how Nana was supposed to be babysitting me, but she secretly tried to take me to her family's church to have me baptized as a Catholic. Mom and Dad were spitting mad, but they'd raced there in time to stop it, with Grandma Yvette, who'd been babysitting Joseph, along for the ride. "I told you we're raising her Jewish," Joseph told me Mom had yelled at her own mom, snatching me out of her arms (Joseph also liked to tell me that they'd dropped me on my head here, but I don't think that's true). "You can either respect that, or you won't be a part of her life." Eventually Nana had come around, but apparently Mom hadn't spoken to her for almost three years!

"There's a long history of people of other religions trying to force Jews to convert," Dad had told me once when I asked. "So we're very sensitive to it."

It had made me wonder why my mom hadn't converted. She was raising us Jewish, after all, so why not? It would have made my life a whole lot easier with people like Grandma Yvette. But she'd always found a reason not to talk about it—either Henry got fussy, or she was coming down with a headache, or I got distracted by cake. Which, really, is the best form of distraction.

Mom's voice broke me out of my thoughts. "Ruby, hey," she said, thrusting the phone in my direction with one hand, Henry squirming in the other. "Say hi to Nana."

I knew enough to mean that "say hi" didn't literally mean just saying hi. It meant having a whole conversation. I took the phone anyway. "Hi, Nana."

"Hi, dear." Nana's voice was slightly fuzzy on the other end of the line. "How's school?"

"School's good," I said. "We dissected a cow eyeball."

"Oh my goodness. Sounds bloody."

"It was," I said with relish. I'd never even bothered trying to be Nana's favorite, the way I did with Grandma Yvette. For one, I only saw Nana usually once or twice a year, so I didn't really know her. For two, she had a lot more grandchildren than Grandma Yvette did. Grandma Yvette had only the four of us—me, Sarah, Henry, and Joseph—while Nana had twelve of us from Mom and her four brothers and sisters who lived all over the country. So my odds were significantly lower. Even so, I'd never gotten the impression that Nana liked any of us more than the others.

"Well, it's good you're learning. You've always been very smart. How about cheer? How's cheer going?"

She didn't have the greatest memory when it came to all of us, either. Though at least she didn't call us by one another's names. Maybe we all looked the same to her. She and Poppy looked kind of the same to me, even though Nana is a woman and Poppy is a man. Both short. Both round. Both with halos of blue-tinted white hair.

"I'm not in cheer, Nana," I said. "You're thinking of someone else." Probably my cousin Brielle, who was around the same age as me and lived in Arizona. I hadn't seen her in years, but we got her family's Christmas card each winter. She was very tan and very blonde.

"Right, right," Nana said. "How is everything else, dear?"

"It's all good," I said. "Oh, I'm starting bat mitzvah lessons soon!" We had to start learning everything we were going to recite at our bat mitzvahs about a year ahead of time since there was a whole lot we had to recite.

Nana didn't respond. She probably hadn't heard me. Her hearing wasn't so great these days, especially over the phone. "I said, I'm going to be starting bat mitzvah lessons soon!"

"I heard you, love," Nana said. I waited for her to go on and tell me that was great, too, but she just started rambling on about how she'd started doing water aerobics, which as far as I could tell was just a bunch of old ladies standing around and gossiping in a pool.

I was left feeling faintly unsettled when my mom took the phone back to say goodbye. "I can't wait to celebrate Christmas with you, dear. Maybe this year you'll come to church with Poppy and me!" Nana had said. Sometimes it felt like Nana only liked half of me. The half that wasn't Jewish.

Except that you couldn't exactly separate the halves of me. It's like the tale of King Solomon and the baby, where the wise King Solomon threatened to solve a fight over a baby by cutting the baby in half. Obviously, that would kill the baby. Just like trying to cut apart the Jewish and Catholic parts that made me would kill me. Or at least be way bloodier than that one cow eyeball.

Mom was talking again. It took me a second to realize that now she was talking at me. ". . . to Grandma Yvette's house," she was saying.

"What?"

She sighed impatiently. "I wish you'd listen better, Ruby. I said to go get ready because we're going to Grandma Yvette's house."

"What? Why?" And then all of her words caught up with me, because it's true: I don't really listen that well. "Wait, 'we'? As in all of us?"

"Yes."

"But you never go over unless we're having a holiday dinner or something."

"Well, today I am. Aunt Naomi called to ask especially that I'd bring you. Apparently Sarah is having some kind of crisis."

Henry finally broke free from our mom's arms, running to his room. "Take off your shoes!" Mom called after him, but he'd already tracked mud all down the hallway. She sighed. "That kid, I swear."

Normally I'd ask her what she swore, which would lead into a discussion of Henry's future, but I had no time for that today. "A crisis? What do you mean?"

"I don't know how much I'm supposed to tell you, but

she got in trouble for writing the new rabbi a very nasty letter in Hebrew school. She says it wasn't her, but Aunt Naomi doesn't think she's telling the truth."

I agreed with Aunt Naomi. Maybe there was something seriously wrong with Sarah. Like, something in her brain.

On our first day of the human brain unit, Mr. Zammit had told us some pretty wild stories about things that happened when the brain got messed with. Like, one man, whose name was Phineas Gage, he had a railroad spike hammered through his head (*!!!*) and somehow survived it, but it pierced his brain and totally changed his personality. Before having the railroad spike hammered through his head (again, *!!!*), he was apparently a perfectly nice guy and a good worker. After having the railroad spike hammered through his head (I think maybe it deserves more exclamation points? *!!!!!*), he became mean, rude, and dishonest, his personality so different that his friends said he was "no longer Gage."

Now, obviously Sarah hadn't had a railroad spike hammered through her head. But other things could explain a sudden and drastic personality change. "Maybe she has a brain tumor," I said.

"I don't think Sarah has a brain tumor," Mom said. She

held her hand out. I slipped my backpack off my back and handed it to her. She winced at the weight. "If you keep carrying a bag this heavy, you're going to break your back."

"Tell that to my teachers," I said. "And a brain tumor is really the only logical explanation." Though out of nowhere, my mind flashed to the box in the basement. Dybbuks supposedly possessed the body—and brain—of a living person so that they could do evil things.

No way, I told myself. That was totally ridiculous. Ghosts weren't real. And even if they were real, I'd been closer to the box, behind it, at the time it opened. Why would it go all the way to Sarah when it could've just floated into me?

Maybe it's because it's a thing from Jewish mythology, and Sarah's Jewish and you're not, a little voice whispered in my ear. It sounded raspy, like Grandma Yvette, and a little fuzzy, like Nana. I blinked and looked to the side.

You are so Jewish, I told myself, trying to make my mental voice louder than my other mental voice, but I couldn't drown it out.

Having your mental voices talking to each other is not a great sign, chimed in a third mental voice. *Maybe you have a brain tumor, too.*

I shook my head, trying to shake the voices away. They quieted. That was good, at least.

Mom sighed. "It's *not* a brain tumor. And whatever you do, don't say that in front of Aunt Naomi." Aunt Naomi was a tad bit of a hypochondriac. My mom sometimes joked that Sarah had spent more time in the doctor's office than her own home in her first year of life. (But she never made that joke in front of Aunt Naomi.) "Come on, get ready."

It wasn't like I was opposed to going over to Grandma Yvette's, but being told I had to and that I had to do it *right away* made me drag my feet. "Why did Aunt Naomi say she especially wanted me to be there?"

"To talk to Sarah. Pick up your feet, Ruby. And for God's sake, take your shoes off before you go into your room."

"You're not supposed to take Hashem's name in vain," I reminded her, mostly to be annoying. But I slipped my shoes off before going into my room to put on different clothes. Leggings were fine for school, but Grandma Yvette liked to grumble about *what the kids are wearing these days* when she saw me in them. "But why *me*? Why do *I* need to be the one to talk to Sarah?"

My mom's voice echoed down the hallway as I pulled on a dark skirt. "Because you're her closest friend."

I snorted in response, only because I knew she couldn't hear it. "I'm not her closest friend!" I shouted back, pulling the skirt up to my waist. One of my temple skirts, it fell down past my knees. "Not anymore!"

"Don't be rude, Ruby!" Mom called.

I wasn't being *rude*, I was telling the truth. At least the way I saw it. Sarah and I might have been stuck together for years, but we hadn't been what I saw as friends for a while. Officially—in my head—since the Incident, but really we'd been growing apart before that. Friends didn't say, after you've confided in them that you were worried about your grade in social studies because you had a really tough teacher who put a high value on handwriting, which was not your strong suit, that they'd always thought social studies was easy and that they'd be happy to help you practice your handwriting if you wanted, because they'd always gotten A-pluses on handwriting assignments. Friends just gave you sympathetic hugs and told you that you were great.

I bet Aubrey would do that last thing.

I at least had her, but who else did Sarah have? Sarah talked to people, sure, but about schoolwork or dance class. Had she ever gotten called out in class for talking? Or had to leave Grandma Yvette's early—or come late—because she was out with a friend? We'd always been partners in class. Who did she partner with now?

Something twinged between my heart and my stomach. It was uncomfortable. It felt a little like . . . pity.

Gross.

CHAPTER TEN

AUNT NAOMI MET US AT the front door of Grandma Yvette's. She was as pretty as my mom, which felt less weird to say, since she was my aunt. She had skin the color of cream, with rosy cheeks and thick, dark eyelashes, even though I'd never seen her put on makeup. Her eyes were such a deep, rich brown that sometimes I felt like I might fall in, and her hair fell in perfect dark curls to her shoulders.

For the first time ever, I wondered how Sarah felt about having such a pretty mom. If she ever felt a little like me—like I'd never measure up looks-wise, no matter how many years I had to catch up.

"Hi, Ruby," Aunt Naomi said. "How are you feeling?"

"I have a little bit of a stomachache," I said, hoping I sounded believably sick. If Aunt Naomi thought I was coming down with something, maybe she'd let me sit in the kitchen and sip tea and not have any difficult conversations with her daughter.

"Oh no," Aunt Naomi said. "What have you eaten today? Joseph was always a little lactose intolerant, maybe you're also a little—"

"Ruby's fine," Mom interrupted. "She just got a little carsick on the ride—"

"Ruby can speak for herself, can't she?" Grandma Yvette's raspy voice came from the direction of the kitchen.

Mom's eyes flashed with fire. I hastily said, "You know what? My stomach feels better now. Weird."

Mom's eyes flicked to me. "Yeah, weird."

"I'm glad to hear it," Aunt Naomi said, flashing me a wide smile full of white teeth. "Let me know if you start feeling down again. I have some ibuprofen in my purse."

She had an entire *pharmacy* in her purse. "Thanks!"

Aunt Naomi jerked her head toward the stairs. "Hey, Sarah's in the den. Maybe you could go . . . keep her company?" She looked at me hopefully.

Inside, I sighed. But I also noted the purple bags beneath Aunt Naomi's eyes, unusually dark against her pale skin. Like she'd been up all night thinking. Or worrying. "Sure." I stepped around her toward the stairs, but Grandma Yvette stepped in the way. The smell of smoke wafted toward me.

"Ruby, a word." She motioned me through the kitchen into the dining room, then leaned over me and planted a dry kiss on my forehead. "First, hello."

"Hi, Grandma."

"Grandma needs your help with something, my dear." She stepped back, looking at me sympathetically. "Sarah's going through a difficult time. I'd like for you to talk her through it. She needs help from a close friend."

Again with the friend thing. But it wasn't like I could tell my grandma that her favorite grandchild wasn't my friend. "I can do that," I said eagerly. I wanted her to trust me and think this was a good idea. That was how I could be better. It might be hard and take some work, but I could do it.

"Thank you," said Grandma Yvette. She took a deep breath. "We need to make sure Sarah doesn't go off the path."

"Off the path?" It sounded like we were out for a hike or something and Grandma Yvette was warning her not to venture into the woods where she might get lost.

As it turned out, it was kind of like that, only meta-phorical. "You know that I grew up in the Bronx, which is part of New York City," Grandma Yvette said. I hadn't actually known that, but I was glad I did now. "In a very Jewish neighborhood with my parents and my three sisters. I was a good girl. I always listened to my father and my mother, and I went to synagogue every week, and I kept all of the laws and commands. I studied literature in college, and as soon as I graduated I married your grandfather and kept our home and raised our children. I followed the traditions of my grandfathers and their grandfathers and their grandfathers before them, and everything in my life has been a blessing."

Sounded kind of boring if you asked me. (She didn't.)

Her lips thinned a little bit as she looked at me, as if she could tell what I was thinking. Or maybe it was that she was thinking about me, that I wasn't a blessing the way she deserved. "My sister Mary Jane went off the path. She flouted our traditions, and she left college before she graduated, and took up with a Christian boy. They had children and never married, and then he left her in poverty. She died living hand to mouth, and none of her children wanted anything to do with her."

Well, that sounded terrible. But it wasn't like you could

blame that on not following all of Grandma Yvette's rules and strictures, because there were plenty of people who didn't who also had very happy lives. Like my mom. And most of the people I knew, actually. It sounded like Great-Aunt Mary Jane just had some bad luck.

I had to stop thinking about it, because Grandma Yvette had started talking again. "And that wasn't even the worst of it. There was another girl I heard stories about, who rebelled against her family, who refused to obey her mother and her father, who wanted more than she deserved," she said. "And she *died*."

I couldn't help almost laughing. Fortunately, I managed to turn it into a snort. Even at that, Grandma Yvette's eyes narrowed, her nostrils flaring open like a dragon about to spit fire. "Don't worry," I said hastily. "I'll try to keep Sarah on the path."

Grandma Yvette nodded. "Good. I'm counting on you." She placed a hand on my shoulder, and looked down at me, and there it was: *the smile*. A real one, one full of pride and warmth and love. I basked in it the way I basked in the sun shining brightly on me after I've left the dark school hallways for the day.

She leaned down farther and enveloped me in a smoky, perfumed hug. She cradled me close to her, and for some weird reason I almost wanted to cry, because I just felt so loved. "Thank you so very much, dear," she said. "You're being such a great help."

I didn't even care that she was talking to me like a little kid. I glowed with pride as Grandma Yvette stood up, then spun me gently and pointed me back toward the stairs. "Sarah's down in the den."

I didn't say I already knew that, just nodded. Sarah was indeed downstairs. She sat on the couch, facing Gus's chair. Facing Gus, too. She wasn't reading a book or scrolling through her phone, just looking at him. It was like they were having a staring contest.

"He doesn't have eyelids, and his eyeballs are glass," I said.

She blinked. "What?"

"And you just lost," I said. She turned to me, looking confused. "Never mind," I said before she could say *what?* again. "So, uh . . . how are you doing?"

She cocked her head, not looking any less confused. She looked different, I realized, but it took me a second to realize why.

Sarah almost always had her hair tied back. For dance, she slicked it back into a tight ballet bun. For school and after school, she usually tied it back into a ponytail. "It's more practical this way," she told me once, when I asked her why. "It doesn't get in my face. And it's easy to deal with." I asked her why she didn't just cut it short then, but she just shook her head at me like I couldn't possibly understand her reasoning.

But today? It fell in waves around her face. Frizzy waves, too. Her hair was really long, like, down past her chest. I hadn't realized how long it was before.

"Your hair looks . . . different," I said.

She sat up straighter. That was another strange thing: that she'd been slumped over enough where she *could* sit up straighter. Mom and Dad and Grandma Yvette had lectured me enough about how I should have perfect posture like Sarah to notice. "Thanks," she said. "That constant ponytail was giving me a headache."

"Yeah, I'll bet." I stared at her. She stared at me. She wasn't blinking this time, so I looked down at the table, which was covered in glossy food magazines with photos of fat Christmas hams decorating the front. We couldn't even eat ham. At least not at Grandma Yvette's house. She—and Sarah's family—kept kosher, which meant they abided by a whole bunch of Jewish dietary laws around their eating. Like not eating any form of pork or shellfish, or mixing meat and dairy.

My family decidedly did not. I mean, my dad's favorite food is bacon, no matter that he didn't grow up eating it. I might think bacon is kind of overrated (don't hate), but I do love my shrimp. Shrimp teriyaki, and fried shrimp, and shrimp scampi, and—

Okay, I was thinking about shrimp to distract myself from Sarah. And now I was hungry. It was a sad hunger, too, because there was zero chance of getting shrimp anytime soon at Grandma Yvette's house. "Soooooo . . ." I said, trailing off like the perfect thing to say might magically come to me. But the only thing that came to mind was the conversation I'd had with Nana about Christmas, maybe because I was staring at that fat Christmas ham on the magazine. "I talked to my Nana today about Christmas."

She blinked at me. "Christmas?"

"Yeah. Christmas." I felt weirdly defensive, like yeah, I could be Jewish and still go to a Christmas dinner. "My mom's side of the family is already preparing. It's a big deal every year when we go over and have dinner with them."

She didn't respond, just stared at me with her forehead scrunched in thought. I scratched my head. There was my one topic of conversation. Now it was up to her. "Soooo, how are you doing?"

She tossed her hair. Even though it was loose, it didn't move all that much. It was just a solid mass of frizz that drifted a little bit in the air and then settled back down. "My mom asked you to talk to me, didn't she?"

I mean, technically she'd just pointed me downstairs. It was my own mom and Grandma Yvette who'd specifically asked me. "Not really. I think everyone's just a little worried about you."

Sarah rolled her eyes, which made me do a double take. It was an extremely un-Sarah-like thing to do. "They're so worried about me because I wrote one bad letter?"

So she was admitting it. At least to me. "Well, it was a *pretty* bad letter," I said cautiously, eyeing her like she was a strange dog—who would *probably* be nice and let me pet him, but also might snap and take off a finger or two. "You skipped out on your own club, too. And then there's the whole fire alarm thing."

"They don't know about that, though. They think I just forgot about Junior Sisterhood. And they aren't totally sure I wrote that letter. My mom doesn't want to believe it."

I leaned in closer, because at least one of the grown-ups was probably listening at the top of the staircase. All three of them might actually be there, pressed up against the wall, silently battling for space—Mom kicking away Grandma Yvette's foot, Grandma Yvette "accidentally" pushing my mom to the side so that she stumbled, Aunt Naomi furiously and silently trying to shush them. I giggled.

"What's so funny?" Sarah asked.

I shook my head. "Nothing. Just picturing something," I whispered. "Sarah, did you really set off the fire alarm?"

She blinked at me, then nodded. I blinked back at her in response. In surprise. "Why?"

She hesitated for a second, then shrugged. "Because it seemed fun. And I didn't feel like taking my language arts test."

"Sarah, that's *really bad*." My voice was starting to rise, so I leaned in closer, pinching it back into a whisper. "Do you know how much trouble you could've gotten in?"

"Not that much. We're only eleven."

I cocked my head. "We're *twelve*, Sarah. You were so excited about turning twelve you started a countdown to your bat mitzvah. How do you—"

"It was a slip of the tongue," she said defensively. "Anyway, eleven or twelve, it doesn't matter. We're still under eighteen. They won't throw us in jail. If I get caught, so what? I'll get yelled at or whatever."

My eyebrows pinched together all on their own. I thought I felt the beginnings of a headache clawing their way out from my cerebellum (the second-largest part of the human brain). "Sarah, you could actually get arrested," I whispered. "Don't you remember the assembly? I even googled it after to make sure they weren't just trying to scare us. It was true. She didn't just get arrested and fined, like, hundreds of dollars, she got expelled from school and had to go to one of those schools for troublemakers."

The color was slowly draining out of Sarah's face as I spoke. "I forgot that," she whispered back.

I fought the urge to stamp my foot in frustration. "You're being so weird!"

"I'm not being weird. If anything, I'm being less weird." She sat back, defiantly crossing her arms. "I thought you were so sick of the perfect Sarah. Well, here's the less perfect Sarah. Enjoy."

My mouth dropped open so far I thought my jaw might actually kiss my neck. Was Sarah really doing all this because of *me*? Because of what I'd said?

I should listen to Aubrey. I should apologize. But as I prepared to say "sorry," a sick feeling rose in my stomach.

It was too hard.

"Maybe I shouldn't have said all that stuff," I said. That

was kind of an apology, right? "But if you want to rebel, this isn't the way to do it. You don't want to get *arrested*. Or be mean to people." I thought about how Rabbi Ellen might react to reading Sarah's letter. I mean, she probably wouldn't be too obvious about it, because she'd been a teacher before and teachers had to be tough or they'd get eaten alive. But how could reading that mean stuff not upset her? "If you want to rebel, it's about doing something for you."

She let out a short, sharp laugh. "I'm not used to being bad at things, but I'm apparently very bad at being less perfect."

I matched it with a laugh of my own. It was a real one, though. That might have been the funniest thing Sarah had ever said. "Well, you have to be careful, or you can get in real trouble."

There was a strange light in her eyes. It was like the opposite of the light that had sparked there when she was watching Rabbi Ellen speak. "Maybe you can help me. So that I don't get arrested or anything. Or at least so I don't get in trouble."

Me, help Sarah rebel? Be less perfect?

On the one hand, I wasn't sure if I loved the idea of spending more time—on purpose—with Sarah. But on the other hand . . . if she rebelled, if she really became less perfect . . . maybe it would make her fall in Grandma Yvette's eyes. Maybe there would be more room for me, and she'd love me more.

I gave her a jerky nod. "Okay."

"Okay what?"

The deep breath I took in filled me up, made me feel like I was doing the right thing. "Let's do it."

CHAPTER ELEVEN

IT WAS EASY TO SNEAK out, mostly because I didn't tell the grown-ups we were sneaking out. "I'm going to take Sarah for a walk," I told them authoritatively. "She needs some fresh air. It'll help clear her head."

The look of happiness on Aunt Naomi's face almost made me feel guilty for lying. Or massaging the truth, because we *were* actually going for a walk. I just wasn't telling them where we were walking to. "You have your phones, right?" Aunt Naomi asked.

"And don't leave the neighborhood," my mom chimed in. I nodded. It was a nod of acknowledgment, because I did have my phone, not a nod meaning yes. I was a master of massaging the truth. "Be back by six."

"Got it," I said. I called downstairs. "Come on, Sarah."

It was weird to have her listening to *my* order rather than vice versa. I was so used to it: *Hurry up, Ruby. Don't go so fast or you'll drop it, Ruby. Help me bring this upstairs, Ruby.* But she trudged up the stairs, her head bowed forward, her hair making curtains around her face. "Bye," she mumbled through the curtain. Maybe she had a petrified expression on her face—from the lying—and she didn't want our moms and Grandma Yvette to see it and realize what we were up to.

I grabbed her hand. Again, weird, because we hadn't held hands since we were kids and Grandma Yvette would make us do it whenever we went out for a walk. "Bye!"

It was cold enough that I was glad I wore my coat, but I didn't need a hat and gloves. Christmas lights glittered over maybe every other house in the neighborhood, red and blue and green and white. Many houses had those wicker statues of reindeer out front, some of them covered in little lights of their own.

I knew that most of the houses that were dark would, in a few weeks, have menorahs shining bright from their front windows. Grandma Yvette had specifically chosen to live here long ago because there were a lot of Jewish families. Walking through, I thought it was kind of funny that "a lot" of Jewish families still meant less than 50 percent. I kind of liked the neighborhood, though. Not just because I liked Christmas lights so much—which I did—but because it was half Jewish, half Christian. Like me. Except I didn't have little spots of Muslim and Hindu families on me, the way the neighborhood did.

Every year, when Nana and Poppy came for Christmas, we all piled into their car and did a circuit of the Christmas lights in the area, exclaiming at how beautiful every house was, even if all it had was a few lights strung along the roof. If Chanukah fell around the same time as Christmas (it followed the Jewish calendar that was based on the moon, so it was at a different time every year), Nana and Poppy always made a point of exclaiming about how beautiful the menorahs were, too.

Nana and Poppy sometimes encouraged us to put up Christmas lights on our house, along with the menorah. "We're Jewish, Mom," my mom would say, sounding tired. "Jews don't do that."

"But they're only lights, dear," Nana would wheedle. "Not giant crosses. And they're so pretty. What could it hurt?"

"Drop it, Mom. We've discussed this."

But that didn't mean I couldn't enjoy Christmas lights. Or Christmas music. Or celebrate Christmas with my mom's family. Right?

Life was confusing.

At least for now, I let myself enjoy the Christmas lights sparkling everywhere. Sarah, on the other hand, had her eyes fixed firmly on the ground before her, watching every crack in the sidewalk. I asked her, "Do you want to stop? We don't have to do this if you don't want to."

She raised her head up and met my eyes then. They burned with an almost feverish intensity. Maybe she *did* have a fever or something, and that was what was making her do this. Or the brain tumor—I hadn't forgotten about that! "I want to do this."

I glanced uneasily over my shoulder. It was one thing to help her along if she really did want to do this, but I didn't want to help her out with something she'd regret once she came to her right mind. "Maybe we should go back anyway. We can plan to do this in a—"

"No." Sarah's word came out quiet and deadly. "If you don't help me, I'll just do it on my own. And who knows what'll happen then?"

Images flashed before me: Sarah going to jail; Sarah

sobbing behind bars; Grandma Yvette screaming at me so hard spit flew from her mouth. *She said she asked you for help so that this wouldn't happen, why didn't you help her?*

I sighed. "Oooookay."

We kept on walking in silence. After ten minutes or so we came to the end of the neighborhood. Cars zipped by along the main road in front of us. "It's maybe another ten-minute walk along the side of this road," I said. "I think. I've never actually walked there before."

There were no sidewalks along the road. We'd have to walk on the browning strip of grass. The wind from a passing car ruffled my hair. I hesitated.

Sarah took a big step. "I'm not scared. Are you?"

Well, I couldn't exactly respond to that with anything but a big step of my own.

The walk took longer than ten minutes. It felt like hours, but when I checked my phone, it turned out to be more like twenty minutes. Still, I was relieved when the big glowing hamburger sign rose overhead.

"Benny's Burgers," Sarah read off the sign. "Huh. I've never been."

"It's not kosher." Sometimes on our way back from Grandma Yvette's, if both Mom and Dad were too tired to cook something for dinner, we'd stop here for food.

Henry loved the little plastic toys that came with every kids' meal. I loved the french fries—they were perfectly thin and crispy and even better when dipped in a vanilla milkshake. (Salty and sweet? Oh yeah.) Mom usually got the fried shrimp plate, no matter how often Dad rolled his eyes at her for getting seafood at a burger place.

Dad loved the bacon double cheeseburger. "That's what I want," Sarah said as soon as we stepped inside, pointing at the image of the bacon double cheeseburger on the sign overhead. It glistened with meat juice up there, the fluorescent yellow of its cheese draped silkily over the sides of the burger stack, the bacon curling up at the edges. "Except do you think they'd add fried shrimp to it if I asked them?" She shook her head. I was too stunned to reply. "Or I could just get a side of fried shrimp and add it myself."

What she was planning was a non-kosher trifecta. The bacon (pork was forbidden). The shrimp (shellfish was forbidden). The cheeseburger (mixing meat and dairy was forbidden because of some verse about not mixing a mother's milk with her dead calf). "Are you serious?" I said. Keeping kosher might not have been an essential part of being Jewish to me and my family, but it was to a lot of other Jewish people, like Sarah and her family.

To them, keeping kosher, eating the same way our ancestors had for thousands of years, was an important way of connecting with our history and traditions. "Maybe we should start with something...less intense. Like, why don't we just get some fried shrimp?"

She shook her head so hard her hair went bouncing all over the place. "No. I'm going to get the bacon double cheeseburger with fried shrimp."

She didn't even wait for me to argue any more. She just went up and got in line, pulling out a crisp ten-dollar bill from the real leather wallet Grandma Yvette had gotten both of us one year for Chanukah. I think mine was still in the box in my room.

"Ruby?" I turned to see Jamilah from science class, she of the constantly raised hand and the eerily accurate brain doodles. She trailed behind a man and a woman who were probably her parents. All three of them held big containers of french fries in one hand and milkshakes in the other.

"Oh, hey," I said. I nodded at the fries and milkshake. "Nice combo."

"The best," Jamilah said, beaming. Her braces gleamed in the light. A little piece of french fry was stuck in one of the green bands. "Are you getting some, too?"

I glanced over at Sarah, who was now ordering. "I'm not that hungry."

"Oh, isn't that Sarah?" Jamilah and I watched as the worker placed a tray with a burger on it. "I didn't think this place was kosher," she said, sounding surprised. "I mean, the meat's not halal, but fortunately the fries and the milkshakes are."

I didn't know much about the specifics of keeping halal, but I knew it meant abiding by Muslim dietary standards. Sarah would probably ask and the two of them would talk for ages about each restriction and why it was in place, comparing and contrasting what it meant to be halal versus kosher. "That's good," I said politely.

"Jams, we have to go," called Jamilah's mother from the doorway.

"Coming!" Jamilah called back. She smiled at me again. "See you tomorrow, Ruby."

"Bye." As soon as she left, I sat down. As incredibly hard as it usually was to resist french fries and milkshakes, I was starting to feel kind of sick.

I personally believed that someone had the right to eat whatever they wanted, as long as it wasn't, like, human meat. (Though I was kind of interested in what human meat would taste like, for scientific purposes.) Except Sarah had spent her whole life not just following her family's kosher rules, but being actually interested in them herself. She knew all the blessings that came before meals and liked to lead the rest of us in saying them. Once, on a school trip where we stopped at a non-kosher restaurant and the teacher had forgotten the kosher meal Sarah's parents had packed for her, she'd declined all the delicious-smelling hot dogs and curly fries cooked in non-kosher animal fat and had chewed on the saddest-looking salad I'd ever seen, a few leaves of wilted iceberg lettuce and a pale pink tomato. So this sudden switch just didn't feel right.

Or maybe it was that Sarah had said she was rebelling *for me*. I just wanted her to maybe be a little less perfect and leave some room in Grandma Yvette's heart for me. Not throw away her entire system of beliefs.

She sat down, the tray landing heavily in front of her. The silver foil wrapper on the cheeseburger rustled; one of the fried shrimp made a leap from its cardboard container and landed with a tiny *crunch* on the table. "Sarah." I decided to try again. "You really don't have to do this. I think we should . . ."

I went on as she unwrapped the burger, peeled back the top bun, shoved some shrimp in there, and smooshed the top bun back on, pressing it down hard. Juices leaked out the side. Even pressed down like that, I didn't know how she was going to fit it in her mouth.

"Sarah . . ."

She took an enormous bite. Sure enough, it barely fit into her mouth. A pickle slipped out the back and splatted onto the table in front of her.

I stopped talking. What was done was done. I expected her to moan with delight, or gasp at how good it was, or do some other exaggerated expression of happiness that would show me just how pleased she was with her decision. But she didn't.

She did worse. She just took bite after bite with grim determination, her eyes fixed on the food. It didn't even look like she was tasting it. She just bit, chewed, and swallowed. Bit, chewed, and swallowed.

By the time she finished, her chin was covered in orange grease and Benny's special sauce. She didn't even dab at her lips with a napkin, just turned to me. "So what's next?"

CHAPTER TWELVE

OVER THE NEXT COUPLE WEEKS, things got weird. Very weird.

Number one: All Sarah seemed to eat was non-kosher food. At least at school, where I saw her. I assumed not at home, or her parents would be upset. She'd eat pepperoni pizza. BLTs. Grilled cheese with roast beef. Ham and swiss sandwiches. It was like she was trying to prove a point to herself. Or to me. I didn't even know where she was getting half of her ingredients.

Number two: She became unrecognizable. Not metaphorically: literally. She kept her hair down so that it hung in front of her face when people tried to talk to her. She started wearing ripped T-shirts and ratty jeans, the exact opposite of the neat skirts and blouses she'd always worn in the past. Even the way she moved was different. She no longer shot her hand up into the air to answer questions during class; she sat with her shoulders slumped and her head on her desk. She no longer strode briskly down the hallway like she was going to be late to an appointment; she strolled slowly and leisurely as if she had all the time in the world. "It's a rebellious phase," Aunt Naomi said, if dubiously. "I went through one when I was a teenager, too."

Number three: All the teachers got bamboozled. At first it was kind of funny to see them raise their eyebrows in surprise when Sarah refused to answer any questions. But after she turned in a history test with the letter *E* filled in all down the Scantron (the test only had options *A* through *D*) and completed her language arts fill-in-the-blank vocab assignment with nothing but the words *farts farts farts*, those eyebrows started scrunching with anger, and it got a lot less fun. They gave her some leeway, but she started piling up detention after detention, and she got sent in for meetings with the guidance counselor.

Because of all those detentions, I really only saw her at Hebrew school, where she didn't want to talk to me. At our usual after-school destination, Grandma Yvette seemed a little lost without her cooking assistant, but

I did my best to fill in the gaps. I might not have been thrilled with exactly how it was happening, but why not take advantage of the situation?

I waited in the kitchen, my hands clasped over my apron. Yes, I was even wearing an apron. It was one of Grandpa Joel's old ones. Sarah and I found it years ago and used to drape Gus in it, because it said "World's Okayest Cook" and we thought that was hilarious.

Scratch that. I still think it's hilarious.

"I'm ready!" I announced to Grandma Yvette as soon as she made her way down the stairs. She was moving slowly, gripping the banister so hard, like she was afraid she'd fall. "What are we making tonight? Anything for the Feldsteins? Cookies for temple?"

"Nothing," Grandma Yvette said faintly, drifting through the kitchen. A sharp, shrill whistle split the air. I jumped in panic before realizing it was only the teakettle. "I'm just going to sit down and have some tea."

She poured the hot water into Grandpa Joel's old tea mug, then dropped in the tea bag. We both watched it bob in the water. "Can I have some tea?" I asked, because even though I didn't like tea, I'd force myself to drink it if it might impress her, but she just started padding out of the room. She must not have heard me.

So when our next meeting of Junior Sisterhood rolled around, I was in a foul mood. Though it became slightly less foul when I entered the social hall with Aubrey after Hebrew school to find not just Rabbi Ellen sitting at our table from last time, but three other kids, too! Talia Weissman from our class, plus Kira Howard and a kid whose name I thought was something like Ellie from the class below ours. I nudged Aubrey in the side with my elbow. "We're growing!"

"Like a fungus!" she said back, and we shared a smile.

Which slipped right off my face as Sarah strode through the door, almost five minutes late. The old Sarah would have raced in stuttering apologies, but the new Sarah just dropped into a chair and propped her chin up on her hands. She saw me staring at her, and winked. I blinked back. I didn't think I'd ever seen Sarah wink before.

"Welcome, everybody," Rabbi Ellen said. "Especially to those of you who weren't here last time. I'm very happy to welcome you all to Junior Sisterhood!"

Rabbi Ellen had us go around and introduce ourselves. The third kid's name was indeed Ellie, and it turned out that they didn't identify as a girl or a boy. "Junior Sisterhood welcomes all," Rabbi Ellen said.

"Except boys," said Talia Weissman, and we all giggled.

"Anyway," said Rabbi Ellen. "I thought that today we'd try a little bit of Torah study. I know that most of you hadn't started studying for your b'nei mitzvahs yet, so we'll start by discussing the story we're reading through most of this month. How many of you are familiar with the story of Joseph?"

I only vaguely knew what she meant, but I raised my hand anyway just to be funny, since Joseph was my cousin's name. Talia and Ellie raised their hands, too, but Sarah spoke without raising hers. "We get to do Torah study here?" She was eyeing Rabbi Ellen warily. "I thought that Sisterhood was about performing the traditional role of a Jewish woman? The way my grandma said?"

Rabbi Ellen shrugged. "I would argue there is no traditional role for a Jewish woman," she said. "Your grandmother's view might be that the traditional role for a Jewish woman is cooking and cleaning and taking care of her home and family, and if that's what she wants and what fulfills her, then I'm glad for her. But as we'll learn in studying our stories and learning about our history, women have been doing all sorts of things and fulfilling all sorts of roles." She raised her arms and used both hands to point down at herself. "Look at me! I'm a rabbi!"

Sarah didn't respond, only looked at her thoughtfully.

The funny thing was that Sarah's thoughtfulness continued for the rest of our meeting, as we discussed the story of Joseph, who back in biblical times had been sold into slavery in Egypt by his jealous brothers and risen to save the people of Israel (take that, jealous brothers). It was like the old Sarah was back as she debated, questioned, expounded. Her whole face was lit up like she'd swallowed a light bulb.

I found it interesting for the first twenty minutes or so, but then I started texting Aubrey under the table. And even better, she texted back. Unlike when Sarah and I used to be "best friends," and I'd text her and she wouldn't even look at her phone when she felt it buzz. Did you decide about the play yet?

Yes!!! she sent back. I'm going to do it! But I might throw up. She sent the sweaty emoji, then the barfing emoji. My old friends in Boston are going to freak out when I tell them.

How come?

We were all in band like my sister. They just figured I'd follow her into it in middle school. They didn't even know I like to sing.

Wow, I sent. It was like her old friends hadn't known her at all. Or maybe it was just that she was changing as she was growing up, getting the courage to show off her true self.

Maybe Sarah was doing that, too?

I bent my head down to see Aubrey's response, which started with I used to want to be just like Clare, except I caught a movement in the corner of my eye. Instinctively I shoved my phone under my butt so that it wouldn't get taken away, but then I realized that it was Grandma Yvette standing in the doorway, and of course Grandma Yvette only had eyes for Sarah, who was talking about dream interpretation and if it could be taken as true in the Torah, since Joseph had accurately predicted years of feast and famine in Egypt by interpreting the pharaoh's dreams.

It was kind of weird. Shouldn't Grandma Yvette be full to bursting with pride right now? Not . . . squinting at Sarah with her face all pinched up like she wasn't happy? "Excuse me," she barked before I could puzzle over it more. She marched into the room. Everybody turned to look at her.

"Grandma!" Sarah exclaimed.

"Yvette, how nice to see you," Rabbi Ellen said. She actually sounded like she meant it, too. "Are you here early for the Sisterhood meeting? The adult one, that is?"

Grandma Yvette ignored her, focusing entirely on Sarah. "Sarah, you can come help me in the kitchen."

Sarah's eyes narrowed in a most un-Sarah-like way. "I'm busy here. We're studying the Torah."

"Surely we can let her finish up here, Yvette?" Rabbi Ellen said. "We'll be done in fifteen minutes."

Grandma Yvette stared at them both for a moment, blinking hard, then broke out into an enormous fake smile.

Which I knew meant danger.

"Sarah, my dear, your old grandma needs your help in the kitchen. You don't *really* want to do all this extra studying, do you? Why not leave that to the . . . others?"

Had she been about to say "boys"? My mouth flew open. I had to stand up to her. For Sarah, but also for the rest of us.

And yet, as I tried to make the words come out—*Sarah shouldn't have to go, we need her here*—my nerves failed. My mouth shut with a snap, and I looked down, ashamed at myself. *Chicken*.

"I really must insist," Grandma Yvette said. "I can't do it all alone, and the skills you'll learn with me will be far more important for your future than whatever it is you're doing here."

I looked back up to find Sarah's lower lip quivering. She turned to Rabbi Ellen. "Do I have to go?"

Rabbi Ellen looked back at her helplessly. The corner of her lip twisted in what looked like an unhappy way. "I'm sorry."

Sarah stared at her for a moment, like Rabbi Ellen might declare she was kidding and burst out laughing. She didn't. Which only left Sarah to gather her things and follow Grandma Yvette out of the room, her shoulders drooping with the weight of her books.

I actually felt kind of bad for her. It seemed Rabbi Ellen and the other kids did, too, or maybe it was that Sarah was the life of the discussion, because we got off-topic into talking about our own dreams and never got back to Joseph's. Rabbi Ellen finally said that we could go five minutes early. We left her sitting at the table, chewing her lip and staring out the nearby window into the sanctuary.

In the hallway, Aubrey and I were met by the sound of breaking glass. We looked at each other, concerned, but nothing else followed. "Where was that from?" I asked.

"There?" Aubrey pointed down the hall toward the open door that lead into the dairy kitchen. Something else shattered, and Grandma Yvette let out a cry.

"Well, that didn't sound good," I said, and for a mean flash of a moment, I thought that whatever had happened, it served Grandma Yvette right.

But only a moment. Then I went back to Aubrey. It had been really fun texting her. And it seemed like she'd had fun texting me, too. "Hey," I said. "Um. Do you think you might want to sleep over my house sometime soon?" I held my breath. What if I'd been wrong, and Aubrey had only been humoring me, and she didn't actually want to be my—

"That would be so fun!" Aubrey squealed, clapping her hands together. "Maybe Saturday? Sunday I have to go over my aunt's house."

My shoulders sagged in relief. "Yeah, Saturday should be good. And it'll be Chanukah! You can light the candles with us."

"Check with your parents as soon as you get home and text me," Aubrey told me. "And I'll do the same."

We smiled goofily at each other. It felt really nice, having a friend who wasn't Sarah. Who I actually had things in common with that wasn't just years and years of being stuck together by virtue of family blood.

"I don't know what's gotten into you!" cried Grandma Yvette in a raspy voice from the kitchen. Aubrey and I turned in the direction of the dairy kitchen. "Go out into the hallway and think about what you've done!"

She couldn't possibly be talking to—but out strode Sarah, looking very pleased with herself. I called, "What did you do?"

She shrugged, swaggering toward us. "Tried juggling with some plates." She cracked a smile. "As it turns out, I am not very good at juggling."

I goggled at her. Her smile grew wider, seemingly more pleased by my disbelief. "Anyway, what are you chumps up to?"

"Just making plans for our sleepover on Saturday!" Aubrey announced. She sounded almost proud.

"Ooh, a sleepover?" Sarah asked. A really bad feeling dropped into my stomach. Sure enough, she continued, "I'll come, too."

"You weren't invited," I said through clenched teeth. Of course Sarah would have to ruin everything.

She didn't seem bothered. If anything, her smile stretched even wider. I hadn't realized smiles could go that wide. It was kind of creepy. No, really creepy. "I'll group text my parents and Aunt Margaret now. Can't wait!"

It'll be okay, I told myself. And Aubrey.

I had no idea how wrong I was.

CHAPTER THIRTEEN

ON SATURDAY I SLEPT ALMOST the latest I'd ever slept. By the time I blinked my crusty eyelids open, the clock was flashing noon! I padded out into the kitchen, my jaw creaking in a yawn.

"Oh good, you're not dead," Dad said. He was standing at the counter, mixing something in a bowl. The squelching noise it was making suggested either tuna salad or egg salad. The thought of either one right now made me queasy, so I just took a seat at the table next to Mom and Henry.

"Good morning to you, too," I said.

"G'morning!" Henry squealed, kicking his feet. He had a plate of carrot sticks and ranch in front of him, because he was a weird, freakish four-year-old who couldn't get enough vegetables. Especially if they were slathered in ranch dressing.

"Morning, Hen." I turned to Mom. "Don't forget, my new friend Aubrey is sleeping over."

"I know. You've only reminded me about a thousand times," she said. "Don't you forget, Sarah's coming, too." I said a very bad word inside my head. I'd been hoping everybody would kind of forget about that part. "You know, I'm glad to see you two together again. I feel like she used to be over here every weekend. She really needs you right now, Ruby. I'm glad you're being there for her."

Well, I couldn't exactly say anything about how I didn't want Sarah there *now*. "Thanks," I mumbled. It was still too early to eat anything, but I grabbed one of Henry's carrot sticks, just to have something to do with myself. So that I didn't feel the weight of my mom's eyes on me.

Change the subject. "You know, Aubrey is a really good singer," I told them. "She just tried out for the school play on Friday and nailed it."

"That's great," said Dad. "Did she get a part?"

"She doesn't know yet."

"Will she give us a concert?" Mom asked.

I eyeballed her. "Don't you even dare ask. Pretend she's,

like, a famous actress you're seeing at a restaurant and you want to be cool and not ruin their night by recognizing them."

Maybe one day Aubrey would be a famous singer and I'd be her friend. That would be fun. She could take me as her date to the big awards shows and stuff.

Mom and Dad made me spend most of the rest of the day cleaning up my room in preparation for the sleepover. Well, to be fair, cleaning up my room shouldn't have taken all day. But I kept getting distracted. Like, I'd go to hang up the clean clothes that had fallen on the floor and discover my third-grade Halloween costume (a frog) piled in the back, and then obviously I had to try it on to see if it still fit (it did) and if it still looked good on me (obviously yes). And then I'd have to vacuum my rug, which was a lot harder in a frog costume, because the giant foot pads kept getting stuck in the vacuum cord. And then Henry saw me putting the vacuum back in the closet in my frog costume, which made him want to play frogs, so we had to hop around the house together for a while until we got tired, which meant I was way too tired to clean for a while.

Though the cleaning process may have ended with lots of stuff being shoved under my bed, Dad still nodded in approval when I asked him if I passed inspection. "Good job, Froggy," he told me. "I can still remember the day when you hatched from that egg . . ."

"I assume it was slimy," I said, with relish.

"Extremely slimy," he said, with even more relish.

Sometimes I wondered what it was like for Dad and Uncle Ezra to grow up in Grandma Yvette's house. Dad was the older brother by two years, and they shared a room for most of their lives—the same room where I stayed when I slept over that one time, and where Sarah must stay when she slept over all the time, though I figured the lavender bedspreads and lacy pillows were new.

Dad didn't like to talk much about when he was growing up. Even when I asked him a lot of questions, and believe me, I could ask a *lot* of questions. "Did Grandma Yvette teach you how to cook? Did you go to temple a lot? Did you and Uncle Ezra ever fight?" He usually just batted me away and told me he was busy, even if all he was doing was watching TV.

I figured I should change out of the frog costume before Aubrey got here so that she wouldn't think I was weird. When I came out of my room dressed in leggings and a long T-shirt, Henry was waiting for me in the hallway. "If you're not gonna wear it anymore, can I wear it?"

I gave him a look-over. He was big for four, but he'd still drown in the costume. Though if it would make him happy . . . "Be my guest."

So Aubrey arrived a little while later to the sight of an extremely large frog answering the door. "RIBBET!" the frog shouted, leaping high into the air on all fours.

"Wow!" Aubrey chirped. Her parents appeared behind her. I waved. "Is this a zoo?"

I rushed to Henry's side, shoving him away as he shouted, "Yes, and I'm the star attraction!"

"If this is a zoo, shouldn't you be in a cage?" I asked him. He scuttled backward on his hands and knees in a very un-froglike manner. He giggled madly—also very un-froglike—as he disappeared into the next room. I turned back to Aubrey's parents. "Sorry about that. Let me get my parents." I didn't have to get them, because they came to me and were quickly drawn into a conversation with Aubrey's parents. Which gave me an opportunity to talk directly to Aubrey. "I'm glad he didn't knock you down. Little brothers, am I right?"

"I always wanted a little brother," Aubrey said. I gestured for her to follow me in. She followed as I gave her a brief tour, dodging frog attacks the whole time. It made the pretty boring assortment of living room and kitchen and bathroom more interesting, at least. We ended in my room, where she placed her backpack on the ground and took a seat on the end of my bed. "Nice room."

"Thanks." I looked around as she did, trying to imagine what it was like to see it through her eyes. My blue flowered quilt. The bookshelf filled with lots of graphic novels and fantasy series. The photo board over my cluttered desk packed with pictures of my family and old friends and Sarah, who was in both categories. I took the opportunity to kick a stray sock under the bed. "Oh, and hey, if you really want a little brother, you can always have Henry."

"Ooh, I wish," Aubrey said. She crossed her ankles and leaned forward. "I'll trade you for Clare. She's been so grumpy lately about the move. All she does is sulk and text her friends from Boston and play her flute."

"That sucks," I said sympathetically.

"Yeah, I guess," said Aubrey. "I was fine moving. I mean, it was hard, leaving everything I'd grown up with, but it was kind of nice, the idea of having a fresh start, you know?" She kicked her feet, coming dangerously close to kicking that sock back out. "And here I am, at my first sleepover since the move."

"I'm honored," I said, pressing my hand against my

heart. "My victory speech will only be about an hour long, so get comfortable."

Aubrey giggled. I smiled. This was already so different from my past sleepovers with Sarah. I liked just sitting around and talking like this, but Sarah always wanted to be doing some kind of activity. Learning origami. Drawing the bowl of fruit sitting on the kitchen table. Practicing trivia questions to "keep our brains sharp." "This is my first non-Sarah sleepover in a while, too," I said. "Besides, like, birthday parties and stuff where I'd have a bunch of people over."

"Oh man, does that mean I'm going to have to give a victory speech, too?"

We laughed again. I slid off my chair and stretched out on the rug. She laid back on my bed. And we just talked, and talked, and talked. She told me about why her family moved here—because her dad, who'd spent most of his life working at other people's restaurants, finally received the investment to start a restaurant of his own in the area. I couldn't wait to eat there. I told her about my past with Sarah, and especially one sleepover where she'd told me about Rube Goldberg, who was this guy who built these elaborate, complicated machines to do mundane tasks like turning on a light or putting food on a plate, and he was Jewish, which was always a fun point of connection, so we'd spent literally the entire night crafting this enormous contraption that ran through the living room, pulling strings and pushing balls, that would ultimately pour us glasses of orange juice for breakfast in the morning. (But it had actually turned out to pour us large amounts of orange juice all over the kitchen table. We'd laughed and laughed and laughed.)

That had been really fun.

So by the time Sarah texted me that she was here, I actually wasn't annoyed at seeing her. That nice feeling lasted through dinner, when Mom and Dad ordered some pizzas—sausage and onion for me and Aubrey, plain cheese for Sarah and also me, because I could put away a lot of pizza—and let us eat in the living room. After dinner, we lit the menorah together, singing the blessings as a group. Well, mostly singing. Henry—who'd dropped a big glob of tomato sauce on my old costume—ribbeted. Mom and Dad gave each of us a little friendship bracelet kit as a present, then went to go put Henry to bed, leaving the three of us girls to shelter in my room from what would probably soon be a naked, wet four-year-old shedding bubbles all over the house.

"What else did you get for Chanukah?" Aubrey asked

us. I'd gotten a slime kit and some gift cards from Mom and Dad, which I told her about, but I wouldn't get anything else until our family Chanukah party on the eighth night. I looked over to Sarah to answer next. Instead, she asked a question of her own.

"You tried out for the musical, right? How did it go?"

There was the old Sarah peeking through this new Sarah: always thoughtful. Sometimes I thought she had notecards of what each person in her life cared about and practiced with them before she went to bed. Or maybe she was just naturally thoughtful. Either way.

Aubrey lit up like a string of Christmas lights. "It went really well! I sang my song perfectly and nailed the dance audition!"

I smiled proudly at her. "She's going to be Belle."

Aubrey giggled. "No way. Like I said, Belle's going to be an eighth grader." She scratched her head nervously, her smile fading. "I just hope I at least get into the chorus. I'm really nervous."

"Don't worry," Sarah said. "I'm sure you'll do great."

Aubrey chewed her lip. Then leaned back. "What should we do now? Should we try making some friendship bracelets?"

"I have a better idea." Sarah's voice sounded cold.

"What's your better idea?" I asked her.

"We're going to sneak out and have some fun."

I boggled at her. Aubrey goggled at her. Those were both incredibly fun words. "What are you talking about? Sneak out where?"

The issue with sneaking out of my house isn't that I was so afraid of my parents' reactions or worried about what would happen to me alone in the dark, but . . . that there wasn't anything to do. It wasn't like we could take a car and drive somewhere, and the only things within a couple miles were more houses. Or trees. Our own house was at the end of a long subdivision, with streets winding in on themselves. None of our friends lived in the neighborhood, either. Well, Joey Ramirez did, somewhere near the beginning, but I knew that only because we used to trick-or-treat together when we were little kids. Now he was ew.

"You'll see," Sarah said mysteriously. "I brought a surprise with me." She nodded toward her bag, which now looked more interesting than a hot-pink school backpack had any right to look. She hadn't even covered it with any cool patches or pins. "We should change into black clothes. Ooh, maybe do those black streaks on our cheeks you always see in movies."

"I don't know if I have any of that stuff," I said cautiously.

Sarah was already pulling a pair of black leggings and a long-sleeved black tee out of her bag, then a pair of black gloves and a black knitted cap she pulled down tight over her ears. I looked away while she was changing, but that didn't make it any less weird that she was doing it right in front of me and Aubrey. Sarah *always* excused herself to the bathroom to change. Even in the locker room. "What are you guys waiting for?" she said.

I didn't move. "For my parents to go to sleep, for one," I said. Sarah's shoulders sagged.

"Right. I didn't think about that."

"And to find out what we're doing out there, for two." I crossed my arms. Aubrey did the same, which kind of made me feel like we were a team with a uniform of crossed arms. "Because if my parents find out we snuck out in the middle of the night, I'm going to get in *huuuuge* trouble. So whatever it is, it has to be worth it."

When Sarah didn't reply right away, Aubrey chimed in. "Maybe we should just get in pj's and watch a movie. There's supposed to be a really good one on—"

"I have to do this with or without you," Sarah interrupted. Aubrey and I both fell silent. I didn't know what

Aubrey was doing, but I was examining Sarah's face. I had no idea what I was looking for. Maybe some sign that she had a real important plan? Whatever it was, I didn't find it. Just a spray of little pimples on her forehead and an almost feverish shine to her eyes. "You can stay here if you want."

"Okay," Aubrey said quickly, sounding relieved, but I didn't say anything. Not yet. After all, my parents, and Aunt Naomi, and Grandma Yvette, they had all asked me to help Sarah. To keep an eye on her. To talk to her and make sure she was okay. Was I really doing that if I let her walk out into the dark, cold night all alone?

Go and help her, part of me whispered in my head. Because I wanted to help Sarah be "bad," right? I'd even told her I would help. Well, this was shaping up to be pretty "bad" of her. Way worse than eating some shrimp and cheeseburgers.

So yeah. I had to do this.

And you know what? It was wrong, and I knew it. My parents would be really mad at me. I knew I shouldn't be doing it.

And that just made it all the more thrilling.

CHAPTER FOURTEEN

SARAH REFUSED TO TELL US anything more. "You'll see," she kept saying, even as I changed into black jeans and a black sweater. I did have to wear a gray jacket, which hopefully wouldn't be our downfall. "Nothing dangerous. I just have something I need to do."

"Was this why you wanted to sleep over here?" I asked her. We had a movie playing, the one Aubrey'd wanted to see, but none of us were actually watching it. Somebody was even getting stabbed, which normally would've made me pay attention.

Sarah looked over my left shoulder. "Of course not."

"You're totally lying," Aubrey said.

"How can you tell?" I was intrigued.

"I can just tell," Aubrey said. She tossed her hair. "She won't look us in the eyes. Her foot's jiggling like she's nervous."

"Shut up," Sarah said, but she didn't tell Aubrey she was wrong.

"Is it Joey Ramirez?" Aubrey asked. "Do you want to hook up with him or something?"

Sarah wrinkled her nose. "No. Gross."

"Who else lives in this neighborhood?" Aubrey turned to me. "Besides Joey. Doesn't Jamilah from our science class live around here somewhere?"

"I don't even know who Jamilah is," Sarah said. "Anyway, was that your parents' door closing?"

I checked the clock. It was eleven o'clock sharp. Henry had been sleeping for hours, and now my parents were most likely going to bed, too.

"We'll give it twenty minutes or so to make sure they're not going to come back out," Sarah said. She didn't even hesitate. It made me wonder how she'd come up with this plan. If this was her first time, or if she'd snuck out before. "And then we'll go. Aubrey, you don't want to come?"

"Definitely not." Aubrey was firm. "Besides, you'll need someone here to cover for you. What if your parents get

161

up and want to talk to you or something? Or Henry runs in here and screams loud enough to wake everyone up?"

He was known to do that.

"A lump of pillows in the sleeping bags won't cut it," Aubrey continued. "But I can tell them that . . . I don't know, you're in the shower."

I wrinkled my forehead. "That Sarah and I are both in the shower?"

"I'll work on it," Aubrey said. "Just get this over with so we can actually watch the movie."

"Thanks, Aubrey," Sarah said.

"Yeah, thanks, Aubrey. And sorry to make you do this," I said. I hoped this wouldn't mess up our friendship, but this was really Sarah's fault, not mine. Next time I'd make sure it was just me and Aubrey. "We'll be back soon." That I said with a look over at Sarah, who, again, pointedly refused to meet my eyes. "Soon, I say."

And with that, we climbed out the window. I'd done it before, just for fun, but this was the first time I'd done it when I wasn't supposed to. Well, to be fair, I was never actually *supposed* to climb out the window unless there was a fire or something and the doors turned into fiery deathtraps. But since my room was on the first floor,

Mom and Dad didn't get too mad. They just rolled their eyes at me.

They wouldn't just roll their eyes if they knew Sarah and I were slipping through the black night like ninjas, running through the neighbors' backyards to avoid the streetlights.

Sarah had her backpack with her, held tightly in her arms, but I carried nothing with me but my phone and my keys, just in case. I said, "Are you going to tell me what you have in there?"

She didn't slow down at all. "No."

"Ooookay." We sailed through the Perettis' backyard, the Stilwells', the Chiangs'. Then we turned a corner, and I didn't know whose backyards we were trespassing in. A cold wind whipped through my hair, making me shiver. Sarah had made at least one good decision tonight by wearing that hat. "We're not leaving the neighborhood, right?" There wasn't much else out there, but that didn't mean this new Sarah didn't have some horrible dark witch ritual she wanted to do in the dead of night in the middle of the woods . . .

She shook her head. *Phew.* "We're almost there, actually," she said. She squinted at the back of a house we were passing. "We should probably go around front so I can see the house numbers."

I followed her through the house's side yard. Dead grass crunched under my feet, and the fence door creaked open. "Does anyone even live here?" I murmured to Sarah as we rounded toward the front yard.

"They moved in recently." She hung back just shy of the sidewalk, so that none of the streetlight splashed on her. "You can stay here."

"Stay here? Where are you going?" My voice squeaked a little at the end. A branch creaked overhead. Otherwise, there was no noise but a dog barking far in the distance. Or was it a wolf? Did wolves live here?

Was I going to get eaten by a *wolf*?

"Wait!" I chased after her as she approached the house and set her backpack on the ground between her feet. The windows of the house were dark, curtains drawn from the inside. The house itself looked a lot like my own family's: a white ranch, bushes neatly trimmed out front, brightly colored shutters (but theirs were blue, while ours were green).

"You might not want to be here for this." Sarah reached down and pulled something out of her bag. Two somethings, actually, one filling each hand. I grabbed my phone and shined its light her way.

I gasped. "Are those *eggs*?"

She didn't answer me. She just pitched the eggs right at the front of the house. Their sharp splats drowned out the sound of my next two gasps.

"What are you *doing*?" I couldn't move. My mouth hung open so wide you probably could've fit three whole eggs in there.

But she didn't try. She hurled three more eggs at the front of the house. Each one smashed open with a crack, oozing gleaming clear goo down the white siding.

A light flickered on. I yelped. "We have to run!" I might have wanted to help Sarah be "bad" for a bit, but not if *I* was going to get in trouble!

"One more second." She leaned back down and grabbed something else from her bag, bigger than an egg. She hefted it in her hands, its edges jagged.

A giant rock. Her eyes narrowed as she looked at the front window, and she lifted the rock over her head, preparing to throw.

I was still frozen. But I looked toward the window. In the new light, I could see a menorah sitting proudly on display, the dull brass already covered in drippings of wax. Or maybe it was that they hadn't cleaned it since last year. My parents did that all the time, not scooping out any of the little cups until they were filled with too much wax where they couldn't finagle a new candle in.

Somehow that memory thawed me in a split second.

"No!" I shouted, diving toward her. The rock dropped from her hands, falling to the ground with a thump. The two of us followed. She landed hard on her back, crying out. I rolled on top of her before she could get up and try to throw anything again. She bucked against me, her lips peeled back from her teeth in fury.

"Get *off* me."

"No." My own teeth ground against each other as I fought to keep her down. "You can't just throw a rock through someone's window! What's *wrong* with you?"

"What's wrong with me?" She went limp. I eased up a little bit, relaxing my shoulders and letting her sit up a bit.

She reared up and smashed me in the chest. "Hey!" I shrieked as I fell back. She tried to shove me over, but the shock was gone, and I launched myself at her. She tumbled onto the ground, her head hitting the dirt with a *thunk*.

"Is somebody out there?"

We both froze, our heads whipping toward the front door. I turned back a moment sooner than Sarah did, though, and that's when I saw it.

Sarah's eyes. They were *red*.

And not, like, the tired red eyes you got when you didn't get enough sleep. Not the puffy red eyes you got when you rubbed your eyes too much. They *glowed*, all of their parts, the pupils and irises and the aqueous humor, the bright red of a traffic light telling you to STOP STOP STOP.

I couldn't speak. I couldn't process it. For what felt like a full minute, I just sat there blinking as hard as I could, like the problem might be with my own eyes, and the eye doctor might have to go in there and slice them open, just like I'd done to the cow eyeball . . .

I had to be seeing things. This couldn't be reality.

And yet Sarah turned back to me and stared right into my eyes with her glowing red ones, and it looked like they were on fire, and even though I knew we were supposed to be hiding out here—

"Ahhhhhh!"

I screamed.

The rest of the night had the feel of a dream. Another light flicked on in the house. I could hear voices behind the window, confused adult voices, a man and a woman whose words I couldn't hear but whose voices practically vibrated *Should we call the police?*

I stared at the window for a moment, like looking at it would help me hear the voices better, and then flicked my eyes back to Sarah, who was blinking back at me with brown eyes. Her own eyes. Her own perfectly normal eyes.

"Why'd you do that?" she hissed. "Get off me! We have to run!"

The voices grew louder. I could now hear distinct words seeping through the walls. *Worried ... heard ... before ... check ...*

I couldn't get caught here. My parents would freak out.

I leapt off Sarah, not realizing I was shaking until I stumbled over nothing but bare dirt. Sarah took charge. She slung her backpack over one shoulder with one hand and grabbed my arm with the other, pulling me along behind her as she raced into the backyard. And I mean really pulling—I had to run the fastest I'd ever run to keep up with her, way faster than I'd ever run the mile in gym class, and it still felt like she might pull my arm out of my socket. I tried to ask her what had happened when we were safely several houses away, hidden in their backyard by trees, but she didn't even turn her head, she was so set on making it back to our house.

Aubrey was practically hanging out the window waiting for us, her waist folded over the ledge. I worried she'd fall out. She helped pull us in, and I collapsed on my rug, so full of relief it pushed everything else out of my body.

And then I remembered the red eyes. I glanced over at Sarah. She'd tossed her backpack on the floor and was pulling off her hat and gloves. Her eyes still looked totally normal, if intent. "Sarah?" I said tentatively. "Do you . . . feel okay?"

She didn't even look at me. "Yeah, except that you didn't let me finish."

Invisible spines bristled all over my back. "You wanted to throw a rock through someone's window. Of course I didn't let you finish."

Aubrey gasped. "You tried to smash someone's window?"

"And she egged the house," I said. I wanted to see Aubrey's reaction, but I was too afraid to tear my eyes from Sarah. What if I looked away, and her eyes changed back to red, and . . . I don't know, what did red eyes like that mean? I would never have believed it if I hadn't been there to see it, but it had to be something supernatural. Vampires had glowing red eyes, didn't they? And demons?

And . . . dybbuks?

No matter how much I tossed and turned that night, I couldn't make myself fall asleep. Eventually I gave up and just stared at Sarah as she slept, keeping vigil to make sure she stayed that way.

CHAPTER FIFTEEN

OVER THE NEXT FIVE DAYS, my stomach welcomed its newest resident. Not french fries, or ice cream, which would have been more than welcome. No, this was a brick of queasiness that somehow snuck in and sat on the bottom of my belly at all hours, dragging my whole body down with a feeling of dread. If I could dissect myself (an intriguing idea, except for the whole potentially-accidentally-slipping-with-the-scalpel-and-bleeding-out thing), I bet I'd find a literal black glob of it.

I knew dybbuks weren't real, because I knew ghosts weren't real.

But . . . what *if*? What could be the explanation for those red eyes other than something that wasn't real?

What if this whole rebellious phase wasn't Sarah at all, but something evil that had taken over her body?

That was nonsense.

But . . .

What if it wasn't?

I wanted to throw up. All the time.

And I needed to talk to Sarah. Alone. But that proved impossible during the rest of our sleepover—Aubrey clung to us like a burr, chattering nonstop, not wanting to be left alone again. And Aunt Naomi picked Sarah up early the next morning on the way to one of Joseph's soccer games, so I couldn't talk to her then. And school? Hebrew school? Forget it. Mrs. Rosen was watching her like a hawk, and we skipped a week of Junior Sisterhood because Rabbi Ellen was sick.

So I resolved to talk to Sarah at our family Chanukah party. It was a yearly tradition held on the eighth night of Chanukah at Grandma Yvette's house, which normally I looked forward to more than almost any other day (except maybe Christmas with Nana and Poppy, which was equally as fun and had equally as many presents). Tonight there was nothing but dread as I smoothed my blue velvet party dress over my front. As my parents piled all the shiny foil-wrapped presents for my various second cousins into

the car. As I entered Grandma Yvette's house, not smelling only the scent of smoke, as usual, but the mingled
perfumes and BO of a bunch of other (mostly strange)
people. Plus the frying oil of crispy potato latkes, which
made my mouth water despite the situation.

Just walking through the door invited a horde of old
people to swoop over me and press lipsticked kisses to my
forehead along with choruses of "How big you've grown!"
and "You look so beautiful!" I kissed lots of old wrinkly
cheeks. Aunt Naomi and Uncle Ezra were here, of course,
along with my cousins, but most of the other people here
were Grandma Yvette's or Grandpa Joel's siblings or cousins, or those siblings' or cousins' kids, and there were too
many of them for me to remember, especially since they
mostly looked the same—old.

I waited until the old people backed off and craned my
neck around the room. My cousin Joseph was crammed
into the corner near the table of appetizers, stuffing various kinds of latkes into his face. There was a glob of what
was hopefully applesauce on his shirt—gross. I spared one
lingering look for the platefuls of food and then headed
into the kitchen.

The kitchen was where Grandma Yvette held court
every year. No matter how many times Dad told her she

should take it easy for once and let someone else handle the food, she refused. (Though she did allow various cousins and siblings to bring some dishes so that she didn't have to do *everything*.) The kitchen was warm and steamy with the smells of frying oil and main dishes—sweet tzimmes, savory beef brisket—warming in the oven. As I walked through, I could hear everyone showering Grandma with compliments. *Yvette, these latkes are perfect. Yvette, the smell of that brisket is making me drool. Yvette, I hope you're making your famous raspberry thumbprints, because I brought pockets big enough to sneak a bunch of them home this year.*

Grandma Yvette looked like a preening peacock at all those compliments, her face stretching out all the way to the sides with satisfaction. Maybe that was why she refused to give up kitchen duty and let someone else make her life easier.

No Sarah in the kitchen. Maybe she was hiding upstairs? I turned around, trying to lose myself in the forest of tall adult bodies, but a scrap of conversation caught my ear. Maybe because it was in Grandma Yvette's raspy voice.

". . . can't believe your house was egged. That's terrible. I hope they catch who . . ."

I spun around to see Grandma Yvette speaking with . . . Rabbi Ellen? She obviously wasn't sick anymore, with her silvery hair fluttering around her face and her stocky body dressed in a smart blue pantsuit. She had a *kippah* on her head, also blue. I kind of liked that we were both wearing blue.

What I did not like? Discovering that the house Sarah had snuck out to egg—and window she'd snuck out to smash!—belonged to Rabbi Ellen. A sick feeling squirmed around the brick of dread in my belly.

I went to back away, but not before Rabbi Ellen met my eyes. And smiled. "Hi there, Ruby. Happy Chanukah!"

Grandma Yvette glanced over at me, holding a spatula in her hand. She looked back at Rabbi Ellen for a second, then back at me, and her face melted into a big smile. "Hello there, darling, come give Grandma a kiss." I stepped up and let her hug me close, press her lips against my cheek. It felt good.

Rabbi Ellen smiled down at me when I stepped back. "It's nice to see you," she said. She held out her hand. I stared at it for a moment before realizing I was supposed to shake it. Her hand was warm and dry, and squeezed mine almost too tightly before she dropped it. "A nice firm handshake, just like your grandma!"

"If only she'd inherited my cooking skills as well," Grandma Yvette put in, giving a little laugh like it was a joke. I pictured matzah balls tumbling down the stairs, a brown butter sauce scorching on the stove in the few minutes I'd been asked to oversee it, salmon with bread-crumbs burning on the top because I'd forgotten to take it out of the oven when I was supposed to. But I made myself laugh, since she was laughing. It wasn't that hard, since I was still living in the afterglow of that hug.

Rabbi Ellen replied, "Everybody has different things that they're interested in and that they're good at. I love to cook, but not everybody does, and that's okay." I was looking at the floor now, but I could hear the smile still in her voice. In the reflection on her shiny beige pumps, there was a distorted version of my own face, a peach blob. "What *are* you interested in?"

Now I pictured my scalpel slicing neatly through a cow eyeball. The strange black bumps on the body of my pinned butterfly that I'd spent a whole hour googling. The summer afternoons I used to spend watching the ants in our backyard scurry from anthill to anthill, sometimes cart-ing around pieces of leaves or crumbs twice as big as their whole body. They never struggled with them, not even when the obstacles looked too big. Insurmountable.

I looked up. "I really like science," I said. Her eyes were brown and crinkled at the corners. "Especially when it comes to living things. I think . . . I really want to do this shadowing program at the hospital sometime soon."

"That's wonderful!" Rabbi Ellen said. Beside her, Grandma Yvette turned her attention back to the stove, where something was bubbling. "I know we have a number of congregants who work at the hospital—doctors, nurses, administrators. If you need any help or connections, let me know!" She paused. "No, I'll reach out to your parents to get things started."

"Thanks!" I said, my face cracking in a smile. A guilty smile. She had no idea what role I'd played in what happened to her house.

Then again, what happened to her house would've been a lot worse if not for me. I kind of wished I could stay there all night, talking to Rabbi Ellen and smelling the good food.

But I had a job to do.

"Have you seen Sarah?" I asked.

Rabbi Ellen replied, "I think so. She's with my grandchildren and the other younger kids downstairs."

"Thanks!" Before she could say something else incredibly kind that might convince me to stay, I spun on my heel and rushed down the stairs.

The den was a literal den today—a den of noise and

chaos. Filling the room were little kids in varying degrees of relation to me that I could never keep track of—second cousins once removed, first cousins twice removed, eighteenth cousins eleven times removed—and apparently Rabbi Ellen's grandchildren. They seemed to be having a contest over who could yell the loudest and smash into the wall the hardest. Gus watched over them, a reproachful look in his dark glass eyes.

I knew that eventually the kids would discover how anatomically correct he was. But I couldn't save him from the sure humiliation to follow. I had to save my cousin.

Who was nowhere to be seen in this cacophony. Unless that was her dismembered leg the kids were using to hit each other with over by the fireplace. I squinted. Nope, that was only a fireplace poker. "Play nice," I told them, but nobody heard me, so I gave up.

Where could Sarah be? Rabbi Ellen had said she was downstairs, but there were only so many other places she could be. There was the foyer, but she wasn't there on the shiny black tile. There was the bathroom, but that was empty (and extremely smelly). The basement was dark and empty. That left the garage.

I pushed open the door. A blast of chilly air hit me in the face, followed by the smells of gasoline and mothballs.

It was dark out there, just like in the basement, but something was rustling. "Sarah?" I said cautiously. I wasn't sure whether I'd rather it be her or mice. Then I thought about Sarah's glowing red eyes blinking in the darkness and shuddered.

Definitely the mice. Mice were pretty cute, actually.

"Sarah? Is that you?" No response came, so I flicked on the garage light. Revealing Sarah sitting on the hood of Grandma Yvette's car, staring at me.

With her normal brown eyes. *Whew.* I kind of wished there was a Jewish version of crossing yourself, which my mom did when she was extremely relieved something worked out the way it did. Except then I realized that while her eyes might have been normal, it probably wasn't normal for her to be sitting all alone out here in the dark and the cold. That *whew* feeling shriveled up and died.

I took a step into the garage, closing the door behind me. Then shivered. The ice cold of the bare concrete floor seeped through my socks. "What are you doing out here?" I didn't say, *Smashing the windows of Grandma Yvette's car? Starting a fire with all the gasoline?*

"It's quiet out here."

That was the one thing she said that I could identify with. The muffled sounds of partygoers filtered through the ceiling and walls in an odd kind of roar, but it was different when you couldn't see everybody. I took a step closer. "Look, I wanted to ask you about something."

"Everybody wants to ask me about something lately." She spoke in a monotone. "I'm sick of it."

I ignored that and took a deep breath. I couldn't just straight-out accuse her of being a dybbuk. If I was wrong, she'd think I was insane. Which maybe I was. "I saw something weird when we were out at Rabbi Ellen's house."

I watched her face carefully when I said the words *Rabbi Ellen*. It didn't twitch, and her eyebrows didn't jump up, which meant she wasn't surprised. She'd known exactly where we were going that night. My face didn't twitch with surprise, either, because I'd figured that based on all her planning. But now I knew for absolute sure.

"Your eyes . . ." I continued. "Maybe it was a trick of the light or something, but I swear they turned red. It was scary. Like I said, I might have been seeing things, but . . ."

I trailed off as she began to laugh.

Sarah has many laughs. There's the soft, highly polished laugh she does for adults or when she's pretending to find something amusing. There's the high-pitched giggle that slips out when she actually finds something funny. There's the wheezy belly laugh that comes along with eye-wiping and a bent-over back, which I've only heard a couple times when she finds something absolutely hysterical (usually a joke I didn't get).

The laugh that came out of her now wasn't any laugh I'd heard from her before. This one was something slow, more of a chuckle than a laugh. Something darkly amused. Maybe even impressed. "I thought you might have seen," Sarah said, and the creepy thing was that her voice didn't sound any different at all. But these weren't Sarah's words, I was suddenly absolutely sure. These were the words of someone else using Sarah's lips, Sarah's throat. Making her mouth flap open and closed like a puppet. "I lost control for a moment. She likes to fight me."

My insides turned to ice, but I tried to keep my voice from shaking when I spoke. "Who are you?" It didn't work. "*What* are you?"

"Why don't you tell me, Ruby?" Not-Sarah said. I didn't like the slithery sound of my name in her—its—mouth. "You're the one who opened my box."

"The dybbuk," I said. Sarah had never been a prankster, but I couldn't help but hope that maybe this was one giant prank. One she'd masterfully designed to show me, through her apparent downfall, of the value of being good or whatever.

But all the dybbuk had to do was make that laugh again to convince me. "Yup yup, you're right," it said. That was enough for me to see it was telling the truth, because the real Sarah would never say something like "yup yup." "And I'm very much enjoying being out of that stupid cramped thing."

So it had been true, then. Grandma Yvette's ancestors had somehow captured an angry spirit in that box, and kept it shut away for years and years and years, until the idea of a dybbuk faded into nothing but myth and legend.

And then along blundered Ruby to mess everything up. As usual.

My mind went blank. I hadn't really considered anything beyond this moment. Somehow I thought forcing the dybbuk to confess would be harder. But why wouldn't it confess to me? The Wikipedia page had said that dybbuks often enjoyed talking about themselves. Maybe not to people who could actually do something about them, but what could I do? What was I supposed to do here?

"You have to leave her," I commanded, but even I could tell that my shaky voice wasn't very commanding.

The dybbuk let out that dark chuckle again. It reached up and brushed a lock of Sarah's hair from its eyes. The thought of the dybbuk being inside my cousin, forcing her to do things she didn't want to do, was a special kind of sick. "I can't leave unless I accomplish my purpose," it said. "You know, we could work together."

"I would never work with you," I said. It had made Sarah eat things she didn't want to eat. Say things she didn't want to say. And who knew what it had been doing when no one was watching?

I wanted to hit it, but obviously couldn't hit it without hitting Sarah, too.

"Think about it," the dybbuk wheedled. Its voice oozed sickeningly sweet, like honey left to drip over the side of the garbage can. "You were sick of the perfect Sarah. And hey, Sarah's not so perfect anymore!"

Maybe it makes me a terrible person . . . but I'd be a liar if I said I wasn't tempted, and I'm no liar. The thought of being the favorite forever briefly passed through my mind. Grandma Yvette laughing with me. Grandma Yvette praising my accomplishments to every visitor. Grandma Yvette hanging my work front and center on the fridge.

But in all those visions, Sarah was missing. And maybe Sarah hadn't exactly been my favorite person before, but I couldn't do this. If I did, I wouldn't be worthy of being the favorite. Helping her be "bad" was one thing when I thought I was actually helping *her*. This was a whole other thing. I wasn't going to help this thing be bad, because who knew what that would mean for Sarah.

"You have to leave her," I told it again, glad to hear how much stronger my voice came out this time. "Or I'll tell someone."

The dybbuk gave that horrible laugh again. Hearing it felt like jumping into what you thought was going to be a hot steamy shower and discovering, just a moment too late, that the water is icy cold.

What if the dybbuk did leave her ... and came into me? Was that possible? How did ghosts actually work, scientifically? Like, if I dissected Sarah right now (not that I would do that without her permission), would she look any different on the inside? Would a black film cling to her kidneys or glop ooze out of her liver?

The dybbuk must have seen the fear and slight intrigue in my eyes. "Oh, relax," it told me. "I can't go anywhere on my own. Like I said, I can't leave this body unless I accomplish my ... thing."

I relaxed a little bit, but not all the way. The dybbuk might have been lying. Though really, it probably wasn't. Why tell me I was safe when it could threaten me with itself instead? Still, I repeated, "I'll tell."

"Who're you gonna tell, Ruby?" it said. "Who's gonna believe you?"

"Everyone," I said. Okay, maybe I was a little bit of a liar, but only when it was absolutely necessary. And for a good reason. "Grandma Yvette knew she had this box down here. When I tell her we opened it, she'll let everybody know it's the truth."

"Your bubbe doesn't believe in the legend of the box, either," the dybbuk said, its voice darkly amused. "Her mother just scared her so that she'd never open it. It's hard to overcome pressure like that, as I've discovered living in here." The dybbuk patted itself on the shoulder, its tone changing as if it was talking to itself. Or to the person trapped inside it. "But we're going to do it, aren't we, Sarah?"

For Sarah? Sarah was pressured? What did that even mean?

It didn't matter. Not right now.

"Once I got past that, it wasn't so bad living here," the dybbuk continued to me, almost casually, like it was discussing putting on a new shirt instead of another living person. "And I realized I might be able to accomplish my purpose while making Sarah's life better at the same time.

It's still hard to be a girl, but it's easier than it used to be. So you should really help me, Ruby."

"Shut up," I told the dybbuk. Or, she. It sounded like the dybbuk was—had been—a girl.

I wondered how she'd wound up in that box.

Saaaaaaaarahhhhhhh. Ruuuuuuuubyyyyyyy. Our names drifted, ghostlike, through the ceiling. Someone was calling for us.

The dybbuk swung Sarah's legs off the car. "This has been fun." Her feet were bare, but she didn't wince when they hit the icy concrete, which again made me wonder how having a ghost inside you might change your body. Was Sarah impervious to cold now?

Sarah went through the garage door, slamming it behind her, leaving me alone in the darkness. But the lock didn't click behind her, so I took a few moments to think. Somehow the dark was helpful in that. It took away all other distractions and let me focus on the words scrolling through my head. My brief Wikipedia research on the dybbuk, back when I thought it was just a shivery ghost story. How a dybbuk was an evil spirit that possessed a person for a short time and left after achieving its goal, sometimes after being helped.

I knew the evil ghost part. But I'd forgotten about the

goal part. The dybbuk had a goal it needed to complete while in Sarah's body, and it had asked me for my help being "bad." That all of its chaos so far—the fire alarm, the bad schoolwork, the non-kosher eating, the eggs and the rock—was supposed to help. The dybbuk *had* asked for my help. Maybe if the goal could be accomplished relatively quickly and painlessly . . . I could just help it so that it would leave Sarah alone.

The big question: What could that goal be? And why was it connected to Sarah being "bad"?

CHAPTER SIXTEEN

THE REASON FOR OUR NAMES being called became clear as soon as I stepped back into the house. If I hadn't heard the word, I would've known it just by the delighted hollers of the little kids. *PRESENTS!*

Everybody packed themselves into the living room for presents, trying not to salivate at the dinner smells coming from the dining room where some of the cousins were setting dishes out on the table. The adults didn't get presents at our Chanukah party, which I always thought was so sad for them. Then again, I'd technically be an adult soon. You counted as an adult in the Jewish religion after your bar or bat mitzvah. My bat mitzvah was going to take place next year. So this would be my last year getting Chanukah presents here. Sarah's too.

As soon as I stepped into the room, the little kids pounced on their boxes, bits of shiny blue and silver paper flying into the air. Then the sounds of delighted shrieking covered up the sounds of ripping and tearing. *Yessss, I wanted this game! Yessss, it's the next book in the series I wanted! Noooo, socks!!!*

I opened a sweater (a size too small) and pants (a size too big) from some of my dad's cousins I barely knew, and a few books from Aunt Naomi and Uncle Ezra. Some little tchotchkes from other, more distant relatives— some colorful socks; a bright orange coin purse; a stuffed shrimp who looked a tad maniacal; a fuzzy blanket. I kept an eye on Sarah beside me to make sure she wasn't causing too much trouble, but also to check out what she'd gotten. A similar assortment as mine, except that instead of the books, my parents had gotten her some art supplies.

Finally, both Sarah and I were left with boxes from Grandma Yvette only. They were about the same size, wrapped in the same shiny silver paper. That probably meant she'd gotten us the same thing. My heart thudded with anticipation as I went to rip mine open.

It was a pair of bookends, heavy and silver. They looked like something she'd had for a long time. Sarah—the real Sarah—would love bookends to take care of all her books. I could use them on my shelf, I guessed. "Thank you, Grandma."

"You're welcome, Ruby." She didn't even look at me. Her eyes were trained on Sarah, as if waiting for her to finish opening her own present. But why? If she'd just gotten boring bookends like me, she'd—

A gasp escaped Sarah's throat. She dropped the last glittering bit of paper onto the floor, opened the lid of her box, and held up her prize: two silver candlesticks. Wrapped in silver vines and silver flowers, they shined brighter than the wrapping paper.

I gasped, too. The candlesticks were beautiful. And clearly much more meaningful than the bookends I'd gotten, judging solely by the glowing look on Grandma Yvette's face.

"My mother's mother brought them with her when she fled to America, sewn into a pillowcase," Grandma Yvette said. "They're Shabbat candlesticks, meant for welcoming the day of rest. Now that you're going to have your bat mitzvah and become a woman next year, it's time for you to have them."

Feelings crashed like waves through me. First—confusion as I realized what was going on, what Grandma Yvette was saying, and not behind my back this time, right to my front, which felt just as bad. Second—sadness, because Sarah was the favorite and this just proved that I could never, ever catch up. Third—embarrassment, because everybody watching this knew that I was the same age as Sarah, and they must all be looking at me right now, wondering why I wasn't worthy of the candlesticks, what I'd done not to deserve them.

Sarah's eyes gleamed. No, the dybbuk's eyes gleamed. It tightened Sarah's hands around the precious candlesticks. And suddenly I knew exactly what it would do. Well, maybe not exactly. But close enough. It was going to do something to destroy the candlesticks: hurl them through the front window; smash them on the floor.

So my dive wasn't about taking the candlesticks from Sarah. It was about rescuing them. I lunged toward her, my hands closing around hers and squeezing tight. She snarled at me and tried to pull free, but I held on. No matter how she whipped back and forth and pulled and screeched, I held on.

I was so focused on keeping my grip—on saving the candlesticks—that it took me a second to realize that

Grandma Yvette was roaring. At *me*. "Ruby, what are you doing?" Little drops of spit flew from her mouth; her smile was entirely gone. "You're embarrassing yourself!"

My cheeks heated up as I realized how the room must be looking at me. They'd be thinking that I was jealous. That I was like a little kid, unable to control myself.

The dybbuk seemed to be realizing the same thing at the same time. My grip loosened enough with the embarrassment that she was able to yank them free, and she immediately set a doleful expression on her face. Eyes wide with a sad sort of surprise, lips parted with shock and pity. "Ruby, there's no need to attack me," she said. "Of course I'll share them with you."

Murmurs arose around the room. I looked around, trying to see if anyone understood. Aunt Naomi and Uncle Ezra looked worried. My parents looked kind of freaked out. Many of the distant cousins were whispering to each other. Sarah's older brother, Joseph, was snickering. At least *someone* was entertained.

And then my eyes set upon Rabbi Ellen, who was standing in the corner. She didn't look angry or upset or worried. Her head was tilted to the side, her two front teeth chewing on her lower lip. Her eyes were narrowed a bit, but they looked thoughtful. *She* looked thoughtful.

Maybe it was the fact that I'd already embarrassed myself. Maybe it was the fact that I knew the candlesticks hadn't actually gone to Sarah, but to the dybbuk. And maybe it was the fact that I already knew the answer to what I was going to say, but I wanted to make Grandma Yvette say it in front of everyone. My mouth popped open, and I said, loud and clear, "How come only Sarah got something like this?"

Grandma Yvette's lips pursed. The room hushed, as if everybody wanted to hear her answer. "Well, dear, I only had one set of candles my grandmother brought over. If I had a second one, of course I would've given it to you."

But her words meant nothing, because she *could* have done something like that. Maybe she only had one fancy set of heirloom candlesticks, but she had lots of other old candlesticks. She had a whole shelf of Shabbat candlesticks that she'd collected over the years.

"You have so many other Shabbat candlesticks," I told her. My whole face was boiling hot, not just my cheeks as usual. Maybe my blood was actually boiling. That would mean I'd probably die. Or else I was a fascinating scientific specimen.

Grandma Yvette's face flattened. Well, no, it didn't—her nose and chin stuck out like usual, and her eyes and mouth were still pits. But something left it, something that kept it animated. Her lips turned down at the edges. Her eyes narrowed.

"Dear," she said, and even her voice was different. Of course it still sounded raspy, from all the years of smoking, but there was something cold about it. Like she'd taken it out and stored it in the fridge. "You only need Shabbat candles if you're Jewish, if you're living in a Jewish household and will be raising Jewish children."

Tears stung the backs of my eyes before I was even through processing what she was saying, though I felt grimly satisfied that at least it was out in the open. That I wasn't the only one who'd heard it. Shocked hisses went up around the room, though the one I heard the loudest came from my mom.

"I *am* Jewish, though." *Come on, Rabbi Ellen, back me up. Someone back me up. Maybe I can show her that she's wrong.* "I'm getting bat mitzvahed next year! Only a few months after Sarah!" My voice broke in half. I took a deep breath, but when I brought it back, it was thinner than before. "I can do the Friday night service for you, practically by heart! I know all the prayers! Here, I can start: *mah tovu. ohhaleka Ya'akov, mishkenotekha Yisrael . . .*"

I trailed off, because it turned out I hadn't memorized it exactly as well as I thought I had. But I still knew it.

All I needed was my *Siddur*, my prayer book. And then I could prove it to her, I could prove that I was just as Jewish as her or Sarah or Rabbi Ellen or anyone else here. Well, except my mom.

Mom. Mom wasn't Jewish. That was what Grandma Yvette was *really* talking about. Because to her—and Orthodox opinion—it didn't matter how many of the prayers I knew, or whether our temple was bat mitzvahing me, or how Jewish I felt, or even that my dad was Jewish by both birth and religion. None of it mattered. All that mattered was that my mom wasn't.

"Men and women are equal," I told Grandma Yvette. Her thin gray brows bunched in confusion. "It shouldn't matter whether your mom or your dad is Jewish," I clarified.

"It's thousands and thousands of years of tradition," Grandma Yvette said. Her lips pinched together. Around her, the various cousins shook their heads and murmured to one another. I couldn't hear enough to know whether they were shaking their heads at her or at me. "And it's just how it is."

I was in it now—now that she knew *I* knew what she thought, I could prove her wrong. I'd actually looked some of this stuff up after the Incident. There were a bunch of rabbis and Jewish thinkers—like the rabbis and people who made the rules at my temple, who'd decided before we joined that patrilineal Jews would be treated the same as everyone else—who argued exactly what I was saying, with lots of research and arguments to back them up. I'd just never had the courage to bring the subject up with her before.

But I didn't even have time to try. Dad stepped forward, a muscle working under his stubbled jaw. "This is uncalled for, Mom," he said. He closed a big hand around my forearm. "Come on, Ruby. We're leaving."

While going to look over my shoulder at Dad, I looked at Rabbi Ellen . . . and my eyes stuck. She still looked thoughtful. But thoughtful about what?

Dad gave my arm a tug. Behind me I could hear my mom snapping at Henry. "Grab your stuff, Henry. We have to leave now."

"But I don't *wanna* leave. We didn't have dinner yet. Or dessert."

"We'll eat at home." I couldn't see her, but I knew Mom's words were coming out through clenched teeth. "All the ice cream you want."

"But I want *cake*." Henry let out a howl, and I knew my mom had scooped him up into her arms. "Caaaaaaake!"

The front door opened and closed. Henry's howl faded

into the outside. Mom hadn't said goodbye to anyone. Which was against our family rules. No matter how long it took, we always circulated through the house to give everybody—whether we knew their names or not—a goodbye kiss on their old, papery cheek.

"Come on, Ruby." Dad's voice was firm, but when I finally looked up at him, he wasn't even looking at me. He was looking—no, glaring—right at Grandma Yvette. "We'll come back when we feel welcome again."

I let him pull me toward the front door, but I dug in my heels when I realized that Sarah was gone. She and the candlesticks. My breath caught in my throat. "Dad," I tried to say. "Sarah—"

"You can talk to Sarah later," Dad said. He spoke through clenched teeth, just like Mom. "Right now we have to go."

"But I don't want to talk to her, I'm worried about what she might—" I spilled words out in a rush, trying to get them all out before we reached the door, but Dad cut me off anyway.

"Ruby, this is bigger than you. You can call Sarah later. Let's *go*."

He was pulling me so hard my feet almost lifted off the ground. My shoulder strained in its socket. I was about to tell him to lay off when we reached the front stoop, and the door closed behind us, and he sighed. "I'm sorry, Rubes," he said. "I didn't mean to yell at you. None of this is your fault, you know that? And it doesn't have to do with you?"

It had seemed a lot like it had to do with me—almost entirely so, actually—but I nodded, because I knew that was what he wanted me to do. He sighed again.

"Your grandma didn't talk to me for almost a year when I first brought Mom home," he said. I stayed quiet. I wanted to hear what he said—he didn't talk much about when he was younger, before he had me. "It was the first big fight we'd ever had. I went to college where she wanted me to go, I majored in what she thought I should major in, I moved back here after I graduated. But I fell in love with your mom, and I defied *my* mom for the first time. It was a really big deal, Rubes. But I didn't give in. There are some things too important to give in over. And you're one of them."

We hadn't made it to the car yet—I could see the glow of lights where we'd parked near the neighbor's driveway; hear the screeches of Henry as Mom fought him into his car seat—but Dad stopped and spun me around, resting a hand on my shoulder, then sunk down to one knee before me.

"Are you proposing?" I joked, and even though the last thing I felt like doing right now was laughing, a bubble of one escaped anyway. Like a little fart. And just like even a little fart can make the whole room smell, that little laugh made everything seem a little lighter.

Dad snorted. "No, I am not proposing." His face turned thoughtful. "I guess I am technically proposing something, though." Back to serious. "I know Grandma Yvette isn't the easiest person to get along with. Your mom and I have had a lot of talks about how much we want her to be involved in your and Henry's lives. After tonight, well . . . I just want to make sure that you know how much you're loved. And valued. By me and your mom, and your aunt and uncle and cousins, and yes, even your grandma."

Something hard rose in my throat. If I said something serious, I thought it might make me cry. "You didn't mention Henry, so I can only assume Henry hates me."

Dad snorted again. "I want to make sure that you tell me if anyone ever makes you feel less than."

"Less than what?"

"Less than anyone else, for any reason," Dad said. "And that includes your grandma."

I almost did a snort of my own in response. Grandma Yvette had made me feel less than Sarah my whole life. And so did my parents, sometimes. *Why can't you be more like Sarah?* I'd be happy if I never had to hear those words again.

Though not if it meant the dybbuk staying in Sarah.

"Rubes?" Dad prompted.

I sighed. "Did she ever do this to you?" I answered myself. "No, she wouldn't have. Because you're one hundred percent Jewish, and nobody could—"

"She did." Dad's voice was heavy. "Your grandmother and I differ a lot on how we view Judaism and our religion. Your uncle, too. As I got older, as I went to college, and joined the Hillel there, and met your mother, I realized that Judaism is less about rules and prayer and holidays to me than it is our history and culture and people."

My breaths started coming a little panicky. "But I really *do* care about the prayers and holidays and—"

"And that's okay." Now his voice was firm. "Different things are important to different people, and as long as those things don't put anyone else down, that's okay. I respect you, and I know that you respect me. Haven't you ever heard that old saying? Two Jews, three opinions?" A smile flashed over his face. "There are a lot of different ways to be a Jew. There's room in the tent for all of us."

"What tent?"

"The tent is a metaphor."

"Oh." We'd learned about metaphors in school. What he was really saying was that there was room for all different kinds of Jews in Judaism. Which made sense.

If only his opinion was the one that mattered.

"Right," I said. "Okay, sure."

He gave me a relieved smile, then stood up straight again. "Okay, let's get home. I'll talk to your grandma tomorrow. Everything's going to be okay."

I glanced over my shoulder once more before we made it to the car. I couldn't see quite clearly, but it looked like there was a dark smudge on Grandma's roof. Vaguely person-shaped, like a gargoyle.

But like I said, we were far away, and I assumed I was seeing things—maybe a large bird or something. Turkey vultures flapped their way around here all the time, and they were huge birds. (Apparently very friendly and sociable, too, though you wouldn't know it to look at them. I'd like to befriend a turkey vulture and see if that Wikipedia article was true.)

But I wasn't seeing things. And it wasn't a turkey vulture.

CHAPTER SEVENTEEN

THE FIRST VERSION OF THE story came through a text from Uncle Ezra to my dad that night, not long after we got home. All it said was, Sarah fell off the roof. Is OK. Talk to u tomorrow

Dad stared down at his phone, eyebrows lifting in surprise. "Well, that doesn't sound good. I wonder what happened."

I took a deep breath and tangled my fingers in my hair so that I wouldn't claw at my face. Is OK. I focused on those two words. As long as she was okay, the dybbuk hadn't done any lasting harm.

The second version of the story came from Aunt Naomi on the phone the next day. "I don't know what's gotten into that girl! I'm hoping I can give her some herbal tea that might help with all these emotions." She sounded like her throat was clogged with tears. "All I know is that she climbed up there and fell off. She won't tell me what she was doing."

Grandma Yvette had a theory, which became the third version. Dad must have talked to her, because she gave me a quick, flat, fake-sounding "Sorry if I hurt your feelings, of course you're Jewish" before launching into her idea. "That dear girl must have thought she saw an injured bird up there. You know, two birds have flown into the second-story windows this year and laid twitching on the roof. Must have something to do with the way sunlight hits the windows."

Meanwhile, the Shabbat candlesticks had gone missing. Nobody was sure what had happened to them. Grandma Yvette waved it off. "She must have stored them somewhere safe in the house before going to save that bird. I still haven't cleaned up from the party." I knew better. I knew that Sarah must have taken them up on the roof to do something horrible and public with them. Maybe they were still up there.

Sarah—or Not-Sarah—wouldn't tell me. My mom and I stopped by her house over the weekend, Mom bringing a casserole for them from the local kosher market, which is what she did whenever anyone from our temple got sick or injured. Sarah was the one who answered the door, and she looked fine other than the brace on her ankle and the sling on her arm.

Okay, so maybe she didn't look that fine.

Mom went with Aunt Naomi and Uncle Ezra to the kitchen to put the casserole away, and Joseph was locked in his room doing whatever teenage boys did when they were alone, which left me with Sarah in the living room. I didn't waste any time. I leaned into her face and hissed so hard spit landed on her skin, and I didn't even feel bad about it. *"Were you trying to kill Sarah?"*

I didn't know what I'd do if the dybbuk shrugged and was like, "Yeah!" I really didn't. So I was relieved when it rolled Sarah's eyes and said, "Of course not."

Not *that* relieved, though. Because that was exactly what I'd say if asked if I'd tried to kill someone. I wouldn't want to go to jail.

But it went on. "If I kill this host body, I'm just ... gone, I think. Maybe I can hop into someone else, but I don't know. I don't need to know. Besides, I like this one, because I can help both of us at the same time."

My shoulders relaxed a tiny bit with every word it

204

said. Not that what it was saying was great, but at least it wouldn't kill my cousin. "What were you trying to do up there, then?"

"Like I'm going to tell you."

Those words from Wikipedia floated back through my head. *It supposedly leaves the host body once it has accomplished its goal, sometimes after being helped.* That referred to the dybbuk, of course. So this dybbuk had to have some kind of goal it was trying to accomplish with Sarah's body . . . and it would leave her alone after that goal was achieved.

"Why not?" I asked. "If you achieve your goal, you leave, right? You're done, and you're out?"

After a moment's hesitation, the dybbuk nodded.

"If helping you achieve that goal means helping you get away from Sarah, then maybe I could help you," I said. It depended on what that goal was, of course. But one step at a time.

The dybbuk bared Sarah's teeth in what was probably supposed to be a smile. Had Sarah's canines always been that pointy? "I want revenge."

I blinked. "Revenge on who?"

The dybbuk wilted a little bit, like I'd killed the drama of the moment. "Everybody."

Okay, that ratcheted it back up. "You can't get revenge on everybody," I said. "That would mean that everybody in the world had wronged you. And that can't be true."

The dybbuk sat up very straight, and when she spoke, she sounded very young. "They *did* all wrong me! They shaped the world that I lived in, and that Sarah lives in, and they made it impossible to have what we want!"

"What *do* you want?"

The dybbuk's lower lip stuck out. "More than what they gave me," she said. "I don't want to get married and keep some man's house and have his babies and spend my life cooking and cleaning." Her eyes glinted at me defiantly. "And I'm going to make sure Sarah doesn't have to do that, either."

"But she doesn't!" I cried. "Things are different now! It's been, like, a hundred years, or two hundred years since you were . . . you know, alive." I cringed. I actually had no idea how long it had been, but I knew it had been a long time. "The world was totally different than it is now."

The dybbuk crossed her arms. "Really? I wanted to study the Torah and your grandma pulled me away to cook for her! Just like she does all the time! Your grandma is obsessed with Sarah having a family and making a home, not doing what she actually wants to do. Sarah was never allowed to make her own choices even before I got here." She glared at me. "So I'm going to make them for her. Better ones."

And just like that, all the dybbuk's actions made sense. She was rebelling against the future Grandma Yvette wanted for her. Egging Rabbi Ellen's house after she hadn't stood up for Sarah when Grandma Yvette pulled her out. Except hadn't Sarah always made her own choices?

Or . . . had I just thought she made her own choices? Because sure, maybe she liked keeping kosher and doing well in school, but *did* she really like cooking with Grandma Yvette all the time and learning how to keep house? Or would she rather be drawing or studying Torah?

"I'll stand up for us, since Sarah couldn't stand up for herself," said the dybbuk. Her fists were clenched. "No matter who gets hurt."

My own fists clenched at my sides. "You have to stop."

The dybbuk let out an unfunny little laugh. "Go ahead. Try and stop me. What are you going to do? Ditch Sarah again?"

My fists opened up in shock. "What do you mean?"

"You have no idea what it's been like in here." By which I assumed she meant Sarah's head. The dybbuk's voice took on a singsong tone. "Ooooh, my cousin Ruby's being so meeeean to me! I'm so saaaaad!"

I wanted to say something in response, but all the words caught in my throat. I felt kind of . . . bad. "I'll tell," I threatened.

The dybbuk snorted. "Nobody's going to believe you."

"My parents will," I said, even though they probably wouldn't. "My family will. And they'll help me kick you out."

"Hmmm." The dybbuk scratched her chin. "We'll see about that."

I focused my eyes into a death glare at the dybbuk's forehead, like they might actually form into lasers and fry it. That didn't happen, of course. What happened instead? Mom and Aunt Naomi appearing in the doorway just in time to see me giving *poor injured Sarah* the stink eye.

"Ruby!" Mom exclaimed, shooting Aunt Naomi an apologetic look. "Stop that! I'm sorry, Sarah and Naomi. I don't know what's gotten into her lately."

"I can say the same thing about Sarah," Aunt Naomi said grimly.

The dybbuk ignored her, reaching behind and pulling a book off the shelf. She opened it to a location in the middle and buried her nose in it, looking very absorbed. She didn't seem to realize it was her mom's address book. Seriously, there was no way the dybbuk was actually absorbed in reading the addresses and phone numbers and emails of everybody her mom knew. Still, she faked it well enough to avoid having to talk more.

Mom chattered the whole time we were driving home. "A sprained ankle and dislocated shoulder," she said, glancing over at me. The car drifted dangerously close to the side of the road. My mom was not the best driver, but she hadn't been in an accident since before I was born, she liked to say. "Aunt Naomi was saying she got lucky. It could have been so much worse."

It *was* lucky, though not for the reason Mom was thinking. A sprained ankle and dislocated shoulder meant that the dybbuk would have to take it easy with Sarah's body for a while. No midnight egging runs until it all healed.

"She didn't say anything to you, did she?" Mom asked. "Aunt Naomi was so perplexed. That poor woman. I understand you'll change as you continue your march into teenagerhood, but . . . this has all been so fast. And so drastic."

"Mom," I said. Should I do this? Should I really do this?

What options did I have? The dybbuk could really hurt my cousin. And us. I said, "It's not Sarah. A dybbuk—an evil ghost—has taken over Sarah's body," and then held my breath, waiting for Mom's response.

She slid to a stop at a red light, then looked over at me again. And sighed. "Ruby, that's not funny," she said. "Sarah's going through something really difficult right now. And with your behavior last night, trying to grab those candlesticks from her? I understand your feelings were hurt, but it wasn't Sarah's fault."

"That's the thing, though." I was already in it, so I might as well just jump all in. No matter how much my stomach was starting to hurt. "I wasn't trying to grab those candlesticks from her. I mean, yeah, I was a little jealous." Or a lot. "But the dybbuk was going to do something bad with those candlesticks. I was trying to *save* them."

Mom sighed again and leaned forward, resting her head against the steering wheel. I winced, waiting for the horn to go off. But when it did, it wasn't coming from our car; it was coming from the car behind us. "The light's green," I said helpfully.

Mom sat back up. We lurched forward. "Ruby," she started, then stopped. She licked her lips.

I waited. With every second she didn't respond, I felt

my hopes sink further. Not that they'd been all that high to begin with. But they hadn't been splattered on the floor.

"Ruby," she said. "Ghosts aren't real. You know that. Your cousin Sarah is going through something serious, and it's cruel of you to make fun of her like that." She took a deep breath. With all the sighing she was doing, I was pretty sure that barely made a dent in all the air she needed to take back in. "I know what Grandma said at the party was hurtful, and that made you lash out. So I won't ask you to apologize. But I'd like you to be more thoughtful. You're getting older, and you need to think more about how others feel."

I slouched down in my seat. I'd kind of figured she wouldn't believe me about the dybbuk, even if I hoped she would. So that wasn't a huge surprise.

But that last thing she said actually stung, physically, like the time I'd accidentally walked into the middle of Joey Ramirez and Kenneth Lappin snapping rubber bands at each other. "Civilian casualty!" Joey had shouted, but that hadn't saved me, because Kenneth just snapped another one at my cheek. It left a red mark. (I may have left the remains of my and Aubrey's dissected earthworm on his lunch tray as revenge.) Like, all I was *doing* was thinking about how others felt. I was trying to save my cousin! But she couldn't see all the good stuff I was doing, which really stank.

I slouched down even more. "Well, you're *already* old," I mumbled. "Maybe *you* need to think more about your driving."

"Excuse me?" She slammed on the brakes. I felt kind of like my brains might fly out of my head.

"Nothing."

"That's what I thought," she said. "On a happier note, Rabbi Ellen sent me some contacts for a hospital shadowing program you told her you wanted to do?"

I sat up straight. The dybbuk vanished from my—well, no, she didn't vanish from my mind, but it got a little bit smaller. "Oh yeah, I meant to tell you about that."

"Well, Dad and I think it's a great idea."

I perked up even more, so much I thought I might float right up out of my seat belt. "You do?"

"I can't think of anyone who would make a better doctor," said my mom. Now I puffed up with pride. "The program's supposed to start in the spring. We were thinking you might want to shadow Dr. Solomon? He works in the emergency medicine department. He said you'd need to have a strong stomach, but I figured that wouldn't be a problem for you."

"Definitely not," I said. "My stomach might as well be a heavyweight champion."

If only the rest of me was able to measure up. Because when it came to Sarah I was all alone, and I had no idea what to do.

CHAPTER EIGHTEEN

AUNT IMOGEN'S HOUSE WASN'T THAT far away—
only a little less than an hour's drive—but we didn't go
there that often. I wasn't sure why, exactly. I tried to ask
once and Mom's face just got all pinched up.

I like Aunt Imogen fine. She looks a lot like Mom,
blonde and shiny with a wide smile, even though she's a
few years older. She got divorced years ago, but she has a
new boyfriend every Christmas for us to meet. My cousins, Logan and Landon, are twins.

They're nine now, which means they're incredibly
obnoxious, which means Henry thinks they're the best
ever. All we had to do was walk through Aunt Imogen's
front door and Henry was running after them. Logan

said, "Want to see this gross thing we dug up in the backyard?" and they were gone.

Five bucks says this ended with one of them eating it.

Aunt Imogen whisked Mom off to go try on clothes or something, and Aunt Imogen's new boyfriend sat down with Dad in the living room to talk about whatever game was playing on the TV. Poppy, who with Nana was visiting from Florida, went to join them. That left me alone with Nana in the kitchen, where she was watching something in the oven. Not literally sitting there watching it, that would have been weird. Just making sure it didn't start burning.

"Come here, Ruby. Let me give you a kiss."

I obediently walked over and let her give me a wet smooch on my cheek, waiting to wipe it off until after she looked away at the oven. By the time she looked back at me I was the picture of perfect innocence, sitting up straight, my hands folded on the table.

"How's school, Ruby?" she asked.

"It's good," I said. "We're learning about the human brain in science."

"That's nice," she replied.

"Oh, and I'm going to shadow an emergency medicine doctor at the hospital! I can't wait."

"Oh my," said Nana. "That's certainly not a program for the faint of heart, I imagine."

"It's a good thing I'm not faint of heart."

She looked at me. I looked at her. She blinked. I blinked.

An uncomfortable silence fell over us. I shifted in my seat. It made a squeaking noise. Should I tell Nana it wasn't a fart, just the chair? *No, that would just make her think it* was *a fart*. I racked my brain for something else interesting I could tell her. Then I racked my brain for something at all. Anything. I finally came up with, "My temple just got its first female rabbi."

Her lips thinned into a line. "Is that so?" She stood up abruptly and marched over toward the stove, pulling it open and sticking her head in to see what it looked like in there. I kept myself from lecturing her that doing that would only make everything cook slower, as I'd heard many times from Grandma Yvette. *Don't open the oven until it's all done, Ruby! Use the oven light! You're throwing off the cook time!* "Everything looks like it's heated through. Ruby, would you call everyone into the dining room?"

I obediently left the kitchen and went into the living room, where everybody seemed to have gathered in the time I was talking to Nana. Landon was gagging, something black and sticky on his chin. Five bucks to me.

As soon as my feet planted next to the couch, everybody's phone went off. At first I thought it was one of those flash-flood emergency alerts, but then I realized that the phones weren't doing that screechy emergency notification. They were doing everybody's normal chime or trill or (in Aunt Imogen's new boyfriend's case) what sounded like the honk of a clown nose. I grabbed for mine instinctively, but there was nothing on my screen. That was odd.

Something that was even odder? Everybody's reaction when they looked at their screens. My mom gasped. Aunt Imogen clutched at her throat. My dad squinted in confusion, and Nana said, "Oh my word," the way she did when the cat brought her a dead bird. I hadn't even noticed her walk in behind me.

I craned my neck to get a look over Mom's shoulder as she scrolled through what looked like an email full of photos. Weird. Why would somebody send all of my relatives an email full of photos of . . . me?

These photos were all of *me*?

I leaned in closer, my chest pressing Mom's shoulder forward, but she didn't yell at me to stop crowding her or anything. The photos were definitely of me: that was my hair, my *face*. But in each one, I was doing something I'd never actually done. Throwing an expensive-looking vase out of a high window (whose vase? Whose window?) while I laughed. Pulling my leg back to kick a surprised-looking, plump-cheeked baby, which was inexplicably lying on the floor. Tipping a tall glass of what looked like pee into a boiling pot on some random stove.

And more pictures like that: me doing things that were unequivocally pretty terrible. I blinked and blinked and kept blinking, hardly able to believe what I was seeing. Because yeah, that was me in those pictures, but I had *never done any of those things*.

Nana said, "Oh my word" again, but it was less shocked this time. And then she went on, her voice flat. "I knew it. I knew it, Margaret, that you were going to confuse these poor kids in regard to their morals. They don't know right from wrong. They need . . ." She trailed off, leaving whatever we needed unsaid.

Poppy did not. He said soothingly, "It's not too late to fix things, dear."

"I didn't do anything," I said, but nobody seemed to be listening to me. Maybe I should've yelled. I would've yelled if I was angry, and maybe I should've been angry, but I wasn't. I felt kind of numb. Confused. Mystified. Why would somebody somehow fake these pictures and send them to my family? Had there been some kind of mistake somewhere? Maybe I was a sleepwalker and never knew it?

"It's not poor Ruby's fault," Nana said. She wasn't even looking at me. "It's *those people*. She's a good girl."

"Those people?" said Dad. "What's that supposed to mean?"

Poppy replied, "You know what it means."

Dad's eyebrows frowned over his nose. Mom stood up. Aunt Imogen motioned for her to sit. "He doesn't mean it like that."

"Then how does he mean it?" Mom didn't sit down.

"Seriously, I didn't do any of this," I said, speaking up louder. Henry stared at me. Logan stared at his mom's phone. Landon picked his nose. "I don't know where these pictures came from, but I swear, I would never—"

"Are you really surprised?" Aunt Imogen's boyfriend, whose name was Greg, interrupted me. He leaned forward onto his knees, his eyebrows raised with interest. "These people have been kicked out of almost every country in the world. Most of the people in the world don't like them. Don't you think there might be a *reason* for that?"

Okay, this was escalating very fast. I knew there were a lot of people around the world that didn't like Jews, and a lot of countries that had either kicked us out or tried to kill us, but we hadn't done anything to deserve it. Like, seriously. Sometimes people just have trouble with people who are different from them, or believe different things than they do.

I could never forget it. A few years back, a man with a gun went into a synagogue full of old people praying and killed a lot of them. I remembered walking into the living room at home one afternoon and seeing my parents sitting on the couch together, their hands over their mouths. Mom had tears sparkling in her eyes. Dad looked like he might throw up.

"Greg," Aunt Imogen said. "There's no need to—"

"No, I want to hear what he has to say," Dad said loudly. Everybody was interrupting today. "Go ahead, *Greg*."

Greg coughed awkwardly. "It's your daughter in the pictures, not mine," he said. He looked around, as if seeking support among everybody else. Aunt Imogen's face was creased in worry, her hands wringing each other, and my grandparents weren't saying anything. "I'm just saying."

Dad looked like his head might explode. Mom's hands were clenched into fists.

"Hey," Logan said before anybody jumped on anyone else. "Hey, these pictures are Photoshopped, you know."

The adults were still staring at each other, but I zoomed to his side. Time to clear my name. I leaned over his shoulder as he pointed out the shadows that didn't line up, the light that didn't look right, the pieces of background that didn't match. By the time he was done, I was kind of insulted that a nine-year-old was the one who figured out the truth. Maybe he and Landon weren't so bad after all. I glanced over at the other twin, who was experimenting with the suction noise his finger made as it popped out of his nose.

Okay, maybe *Logan* wasn't so bad.

"Hey, he's right," I said loudly, jumping into the adults' sight lines. The force of their combined staring sizzled a little on my skin. Still, I forged on, because I was innocent and now we had proof. "Check it out."

It was like a spell had been broken now that I'd broken their eyeline. The adults returned to their phones and looked where Logan told them, and grumbled assent, and my parents fretted over who could have done such a thing, and my relief that I wasn't being blamed anymore transformed into worry about who had done this to me. Who could possibly hate me enough to try and destroy my family relationships, plus have the emails of all my family . . .

Oh. *Oh.* I remembered the dybbuk, her nose stuck in her mom's address book. Sarah's art skills. Of course it was her. I pulled out my phone and retreated to the side, shooting Sarah a furious text. *How could you?*

The response came immediately, without even a question as to what I was talking about. *Merry Christmas!* And the scrunched-up face laughing emoji, then a bunch of random emojis for good measure: the lipstick, the tiger face, the sushi.

Meanwhile, the adults were arguing again. Mom was saying hotly how she'd gone to church every Christmas her whole life, and more besides. "The Jesus Christ I know and love counsels love. Respect. It seems to me like you should be listening to him a bit more."

Greg muttered something under his breath. It sounded like *flood rater* or *mud hater.* I didn't understand what floods or mud had anything to do with the current conversation, until Mom burst out with, "Did you just call me a blood traitor?"

I wasn't sure exactly what that meant, but from the fury in her voice and the way my Dad abruptly stood, I assumed it was a very bad thing.

"Now, now, that's enough of that," Nana said hastily. "Let's not talk about this anymore. Imogen, why don't you tell me about the pies you made?"

"No, we can't just let this sit," Dad said. He was still standing, hovering over the situation with fire in his eyes. "Not without a sincere apology. Those were some horrible things to say."

Nana rolled her eyes. Aunt Imogen glanced sidelong at Greg. Logan and Landon looked scared.

Nana said, "Really, dear, I don't think he meant—"

"He meant it," Dad said. "They always mean it."

Nana glanced over at Mom. Mom nodded at her, frowning. "Antisemitism is not okay," Mom said. "You cannot be racist toward Jewish people in my presence. I won't let you."

Poppy raised his eyebrows. "Well, *you're* not Jewish." He glanced at Dad, then over at me and Henry. He wasn't using words, but I still heard loud and clear what he was saying. *You're not Jewish, Margaret, but your husband and children are.* And it wasn't a compliment. The tone came right through his narrowed eyes.

Something rose in my throat. I opened my mouth, thinking I was going to cough, but what came out instead was . . . a laugh.

And not just a tiny giggle. This was a full-bellied, eye-tearing, fully flowing laugh. I hadn't even felt it forming. Maybe it knew that if I had, I never would have let it out.

I laughed and laughed and laughed, wiping tears off my face, until my cheeks literally began to hurt. I was too Jewish for them, and yet I wasn't Jewish enough for Grandma Yvette. I was made up of two halves, and yet somehow they were both wrong.

Henry's eyes were bugging out at me, his mouth gaping. "What's so funny?"

I glanced around from face to face. Aunt Imogen's was frozen in an expression of mortification. Nana was staring down at the floor and biting her lip. Greg looked smug. Poppy looked blank. Dad looked like he was going to murder someone with a butter knife, so it was good we weren't all seated around the table, because that would be an especially gruesome way to murder someone.

And Mom? Mom just looked sad.

Henry asked again. "Ruby? What's so funny?"

My laugh turned dark. "Somehow I'm too Christian for Grandma Yvette and too Jewish for all of you. Isn't that just *hilarious*?" I stopped laughing, wiping at my eyes again. "Or is the word I'm looking for actually *ridiculous*? Or *unfair*?"

My dad wrapped his arm around me, tucking me close to his side.

"You know what?" Mom shook her head. "This is not okay. We're leaving." She jerked her chin toward the door. "Ruby, Henry, Aaron. Time to go."

Poppy sighed and muttered under his breath. Nana half-leaned in her direction. "Margaret, don't be so sensitive," she said. "Nobody meant it like that."

Mom walked out of the room like she hadn't even heard her. I followed, leaving Dad to get Henry. I could already hear Henry gearing up to wail, "But I didn't get any piiiiiiie!"

Poor Henry. This marked two holiday parties left early with no dessert.

I texted Aubrey on our way home. Christmas was a disaster. So bad we had to leave early. Anxious face emoji. Wait till I tell you what went down.

Her response was immediate. Ooooooh you should come over!! We're having Chinese food! The traditional Jewish Christmas Day feast, which I'd never actually gotten to experience, since we always had Christmas with Mom's family. I used this reason to get Mom and Dad to drop me off on the way back from Aunt Imogen's, but realistically I think they would have dropped me off no matter what. It was the whole pity thing.

I forgot to feel nervous until I was standing on Aubrey's front steps. I mean, this was the first time I'd been over her house. What if her parents hated me? What if her older sister, Clare, was even worse than Sarah?

But then they welcomed me in and I forgot to be nervous again. I oohed and aahed over the counter full of steaming takeout containers and loaded my plate with chow mein and sesame chicken and broccoli in garlic sauce. We sat around the kitchen table and talked about Aubrey's dad's new fancy restaurant, where his plan was to cook the homestyle Chinese food he'd learned from his family, but make it "zingy" and "exciting" (I wasn't sure exactly how to make food more exciting, but he'd probably have fun talking to Grandma Yvette). Aubrey's mom told us about a new art exhibit at the museum where she worked, and perfect Clare smiled a lot and asked me a ton of questions about myself and somehow always knew the right thing to say in response, which actually kind of reminded me of Sarah . . . except I liked it.

Was this how other people felt when they talked to Sarah? Like when she asked Aubrey about the play?

While we ate fortune cookies crumbled up on top of ice cream (the best way to eat them, Aubrey and Clare told me in unison), the Lius reminisced about a trip to China they'd taken over Christmas a few years ago. Clare got up to clear the table, and Aubrey stood, too, grabbing the container of ice cream and our spoons. "May we be excused?"

Her parents nodded to her, and I followed her down a hallway lined with old school photos of her and Clare to Aubrey's room. "You're just as messy as me," I said in delight as I looked around. Mounds of clothes covered her desk chair, papers were stacked on the floor next to her bookshelf, and no fewer than four empty drinking glasses littered her nightstand. Her bed was made, if by "made" you meant the purple quilt thrown haphazardly over lumpy sheets.

"Your room was way cleaner than mine." Aubrey collapsed atop one of the mounds of clothes.

"That's just because I shoved everything in the closet or under the bed before you came." Though it was kind of nice that I'd managed to fool her. Whenever Sarah had come over, she'd managed to find the mess, and would give me a look that could only be described as pity.

"Nice, I wish I could get away with that," said Aubrey. "So what happened at Christmas?"

I wasted no time in diving into exactly what had happened at Christmas dinner, leaving out that Sarah—the dybbuk—was the culprit.

"Wow," she said when I finished, her eyebrows almost at her hairline. "That's a lot to deal with. Who do you think did it? And why would someone do that to you?"

I shrugged and shook my head at the same time. "I know." I grabbed my spoon and took as big a bite of rocky road as I could fit in my mouth at one time, then winced as brain freeze chilled my skull. You'd think I would learn from that, but I just went in for another bite. It was actually a good thing, since it gave me time to consider what to tell Aubrey about the dybbuk, because somehow I hadn't considered it before now. Would she believe me? Or would she think I was being mean, like my mom?

Or would the dybbuk find out and try to turn Aubrey against me, like she'd done with my family?

I decided to frame it as a joke. "You remember the dybbuk box? The one in Grandma Yvette's house Sarah and I accidentally opened?" I gave a weak, unconvincing laugh. "I think Sarah could be possessed by the dybbuk."

I dropped all smiles and stared at Aubrey, waiting for her to take it seriously.

But she frowned sympathetically. "Maybe you should lay off Sarah a little bit."

"What?" This wasn't good. All my effort, and Aubrey thought I was being mean.

"Like, I like Sarah," she said, like the problem was that I hadn't understood the meaning of her original words. "She's a nice person. You spend a lot of time complaining about her. 'Sarah's so *perfect*. Sarah makes me *look bad*. Everybody loves Sarah *so much*.' But you always brush off *why*," Aubrey continued. "Yeah, she's a little too prim and proper and you're not. But she's also *really nice*. She gets good grades because she works hard at everything, even the stuff she doesn't care about. And she always asks me how I am and what's up with me." She bowed her head and looked up at me through her eyelashes. "Hopefully that wasn't too harsh. Or too much. Was it okay? Do you get what I'm saying?"

"I guess," I said. Maybe it was like me and Clare. Where I liked her and thought she was great, but Aubrey, who was stuck with her, had more issues with her.

"It's okay to like her and also not have that much in

common with her. Like, every one of your friends doesn't have to be *everything* to you," Aubrey said. "Like my friends back in Boston. My friend Ella was really fun and always made me laugh, but she was a blabbermouth, so I didn't talk to her about my secrets. And my friend Kate was quieter and more serious, but I could talk to her about anything. Do you get it?"

I kind of did. For so long Sarah had been stuck being everything to me, and I hadn't liked it. I'd wanted to break away.

But what if Sarah didn't have to be everything to me? What if I could appreciate her for what she was, and not want her to be anything more?

I didn't think I could handle getting too into it tonight. Not with the words the dybbuk had said, about how Sarah felt about me, still making me feel heavy with guilt. *Ooooh, my cousin Ruby's being so meeeean to me! I'm so saaaaad!* So I took the coward's way out and changed the subject. "Have you seen the cast list for the play?"

I was not prepared for the squeal that came tearing from her lips. "Yessssssssss!" She set her bowl down and leaned over toward me so that she could squeal in my face, blasting me with a mouthful of mint chocolate chip breath. Then decided that wasn't enough and slung her arms around my neck, squeezing me hard with excitement. "I got cast as the singing feather duster! I have a *whole verse* as a solo! I'm the only sixth grader to have one!"

I wanted to respond, but I couldn't, since she was strangling me. I made a gagging noise. She backed off and clasped her hands together in front of her, her whole face shining as she beamed. "Sorry! I'm just *so excited* and I can't wait to sing a solo!!!"

"Strangle me again and you're going to have to sing it at my funeral," I told her, but I was smiling, too. "That's amazing! I can't wait to buy a ticket for every night and sit in the middle of the front row and give you a standing ovation at the end of every song."

"Don't be silly," Aubrey said. "Obviously I'm going to make sure you get tickets for free!" She grinned. "But only if you bring me flowers, too."

"How about dandelions that I pick from my front yard?" I paused and tapped my finger against my chin, making a big show of thinking. "Oh wait, it's winter. Hmmm."

"Shut up."

But she was smiling, and I was smiling, too. And then I remembered what happened at Nana's, and my smile shrank.

"Are you thinking about Sarah?"

I shook my head. "My Christian family. It's just..."
I wasn't sure what to say. How to say what I felt. "I feel
like I'm just half and half, and somehow both halves are
wrong, and I'm not actually anything *whole*. You know
what I'm saying?"

"Of course I know what you're saying. Look at me!"
She waved a hand at her face. "I get a weird look every
time someone finds out I'm Jewish. Whenever we go on
a trip with the youth group or with the Hebrew school.
Their eyebrows pinch together and they get a pained
little smile. Like, 'did this one get lost and wander away
with our group? What's she doing here?'" She took a deep
breath and shook out her hair, letting it float around her
face. "I'm so sick of having to explain who I am all the
time. Nobody ever just assumes I belong in temple or that
I belong with the rest of you. Half the rest of you have
a Christian parent or whatever, but since you're white,
I'm the only one who ever has to explain." Her eyes grew
thoughtful. "Well, me and the few other biracial kids."

I sighed. "Why can't things just be easy?"

"If there's anything we've learned in Hebrew school,
it's that things have never been easy for us," Aubrey said.
"But you're wrong, Ruby." She clapped her hands with
glee. "I do love saying that!"

I rolled my eyes. "Yeah, yeah, whatever. Tell me why you *think* I'm wrong."

"Because you don't have to be half and half," she said. "Just like I don't have to be half-Jewish and half-Chinese. No, I'm Jewish *and* Chinese. You can be two whole things at one time. People are complicated."

I was already shaking my head.

"Stop shaking your head like that," Aubrey said, flipping her hair. It smacked me in the face. "You *can*. Like, I've already talked to my family about my bat mitzvah. Yeah, I'm going to become a Jewish adult, but I'm going to do it wearing a *qipao* my *nai nai* gave me." Her eyes lit up. "And I'm going to look amazing, by the way. It's blue with gold edging, and embroidered with . . ." She went on about her *qipao* for a while and how she was going to style her hair before circling back to the point. "Anyway, I'm Jewish, and I'm going to become a Jewish adult embracing my family's traditions. You can do it, too."

I snorted. "Somehow I think the rabbi wouldn't approve of me wearing my mom's gold cross to my bat mitzvah."

"You know what I mean," she said. "Just because part of your family isn't Jewish doesn't mean you're any less Jewish than anyone else." She smiled. "If anything, it makes our lives richer, because we have an extra wing of traditions."

But that wasn't what thousands of years of tradition said, according to Grandma Yvette. I took a giant bite of ice cream so that I wouldn't have to answer . . . and my brain froze again. "Eeeeek!" I shrieked, and Aubrey took a giant bite so that we could have brain freeze together, and by the time our brains unfroze, we'd forgotten what we were talking about.

Which was perfectly fine by me. I didn't have extra time to focus on my feelings. Not with dybbuk research to do, and a cousin to save.

CHAPTER NINETEEN

ALL THE RESEARCH I HAD to do into dybbuks was making me lose my mind. Because I had to get the dybbuk out of Sarah without helping it fulfill its purpose, and there had to be a way to do it. I was either starting to appreciate Mr. Zammit's PowerPoint wizardry or I was starting to go insane.

Probably the insane part.

If not, the research was going to drive me insane. Because there just wasn't much out there on how to get rid of a dybbuk, and what was there all contradicted one another. Some sources said you needed a full *minyan*—a group of ten Jewish adults gathered for prayer—to expel a dybbuk from a person; others said you just needed one person to pray as hard as they could. Sometimes a ritual had to be held at a synagogue, or an angel had to float down from Hashem's side to help. Sometimes you needed to perform a full-on exorcism with an empty flask and a white candle, and sometimes you could just pray it away. Or you had to know the dybbuk's name to command it, or pray it out, or convince it to leave.

Some sources cautioned that dybbuks weren't real and that you should go to a psychiatrist.

The one thing they all had in common (well, except that last one, which didn't apply to us anyway)? The person expelling the dybbuk had to be a pious Jew. Pious as in practicing and observant, which I figured meant knowing all the prayers and holidays. So far, so good. But the Jewish part? Grandma Yvette's words echoed in my head.

Judaism says that in order for someone to be Jewish, either they must be born to a Jewish mother or they need to go through the conversion process . . . You only need Shabbat candles if you're Jewish . . . It's thousands and thousands of years of tradition, and it's just how it is.

If my own grandma didn't see me as Jewish enough even to light Shabbat candles, how could a dybbuk possibly see me as Jewish enough to obey my commands?

That thought darkened my mood. I couldn't get a real pious Jew to help me. Not even Aubrey. I still couldn't get over how unfair it was that we were both half-Jewish, but she was considered full and I was considered nothing by my own grandma just because of which parent was born Jewish.

I was still in a dark mood by the time I got off the bus. I settled myself at the kitchen table and spread my homework out in front of me, but it was impossible to focus on the three branches of government when my cousin was possessed by an evil ghost trying to wreck her life, and there was nothing I could do to stop it. So I just rested my head on the book. Maybe information on the legislative branch would seep through my cheek and into my brain through osmosis.

That's how my mom found me forever later. "Bored?" she said from behind me.

I didn't bother lifting my head up to respond. "No. Doomed."

"Ah. Sorry to hear that." The scraping sound of her pulling out a chair. Great. "What are you working on? Maybe I can help."

"I doubt it," I said gloomily. If I didn't count as a pious Jew enough to save Sarah, my mom certainly didn't.

"Does this have anything to do with what happened at Christmas?"

I popped upright, blinking at the sudden influx of light. Had the kitchen lights gotten brighter in the last— I checked the clock—half hour? "What?"

Mom raised an eyebrow. She looked tired today. Usually she didn't stay this late at work.

"Kind of," I said. She'd already asked me if I had any idea who could've sent those fake photos, and I'd told her no. She and Dad had conferred in hushed whispers I overheard anyway, but none of their theories even came close to the truth. "But also I feel like I don't know who I am?"

"What does that mean?"

I rested my chin back on the table. It hit with a thunk, making me bite my tongue. I winced. "Like, I'm not Jewish enough for Grandma Yvette, and I'm too Jewish for Nana and Poppy. It's like I'm in no-man's-land. And it *sucks*."

I jumped as her hand touched my back, then closed my eyes as she moved it up and down, giving me a gentle back rub. "I know. It does suck. But I promise you, you *are* enough. Of whatever you want to be."

I frowned down at the table. It was easy for *her* to say. She was just one thing. "Nobody else thinks so."

"You are enough," Mom repeated. She kept on rubbing my back, and the soothing motion relaxed my muscles a tiny bit. Even if it made me think of someone trying to burp a baby. I could burp all on my own, thank you. Even if I couldn't burp the alphabet like Joey Ramirez. "I'm sorry your grandparents have made you feel that way. But they don't get to decide who or what you are. Only you can do that."

My mom kept blathering on about how I'm in control of my own destiny or whatever, but that didn't mean anything when it came to the dybbuk. The dybbuk was the one who knew whether I was Jewish enough to expel her. And I would've officially been Jewish enough for definitely sure, if . . .

"Why didn't you convert?" I said suddenly. I'd asked before, but had never gotten a real answer.

Mom blinked in surprise. "What?"

I'd never really thought about it until now. "Convert," I said impatiently. "Why didn't you convert to Judaism?"

I wanted an answer, but now she was looking pained, her whole face creasing up, and I was starting to feel bad. "Never mind. You don't have to talk about it if you don't want to."

"No, I'll talk about it. You know you can always ask me

anything." She took a deep breath. "I guess I just never saw the point. I was happy to raise my kids Jewish, because it was important to your dad, whereas being Catholic wasn't so important to me. And I did love what I learned about Judaism. It's a beautiful religion. Very pragmatic. And it's a people and a culture as much as it is a religion, and I think it's wonderful that you get to be a part of that kind of community. That kind of history."

"But you could've been a part of it, too," I whispered. I didn't know why my volume had dropped. It just felt like something between me and her. "You know the story of Ruth, right? She was a convert and she's a really important figure in Judaism. We're supposed to treat converts the same as born Jews."

"I know that," Mom said. "And I did think about it a lot, and talked it over many times with your dad. Ultimately, I didn't want to convert just to marry him. I wanted to convert only if it really spoke to my heart, and it didn't." She smiled. "Not the way it does to you."

But did it really matter how much it spoke to me, how much I loved being Jewish, if the world didn't view me that way?

Would it help me save Sarah?

"I know what you're thinking," Mom said.

"I doubt that."

"Your old mom knows more than you think," she said. She really didn't, but okay. "You're angry at me. You think that if I'd just gone ahead and converted, then you wouldn't have any issues. Not with Grandma Yvette, and not with anyone else."

Okay, I guess she was right, a little. If you assumed she was talking about the dybbuk in that "anyone else."

"Everybody always has that one thing they think about," she said. "When I was in high school, Poppy was unemployed for a while. We lost our health insurance, and had to move from our house into an apartment, and had to really cut down on our spending. That meant I couldn't go on many of our school trips and I couldn't buy new clothes. I got made fun of. I remember spending all of high school thinking, *If only Poppy had a real job, everything would be good again. Everyone would want to be my friend.*

"But it wasn't true," she continued. "If it wasn't that, it would've been something else. The way I had no idea how to style my hair. My schoolwork. *Something.* And it's the same here, Ruby. If your grandma couldn't pick on you for this, she'd pick on you for something else. You know why? Because she is just not a very happy person, and she tries to bring other people down to where she is."

Well, that was just ridiculous. Grandma Yvette was plenty happy. She smiled all the time.

Especially when she was around Sarah.

"I know Jewish laws are what they are, but we've found a very welcoming space," Mom went on. "We specifically chose our temple because it welcomes all sorts of families, including patrilineal Jews like you. You know, if you grow up and you decide you want to become more observant, you can go through an official Orthodox conversion. We'd all support you in that, and they usually do a quicker version for people like you raised in the faith. And then *nobody*—not even your grandma—could say you were not enough."

She sighed. "What am I saying? Of course she would. She'd say you were the daughter of a *shiksa*, or you ate bacon sometimes, and that proves her point. The lesson is, you can't listen to what everyone says. As long as you're happy and secure in who you are, that's the opinion that matters. Not the opinion of a sad, mean old woman."

I had to hold back a gasp. Not at the thing where you shouldn't worry about what everyone else said—that was a message teachers repeated at every assembly and would for the rest of time. Everybody knew it meant nothing, because we could see how much they cared about what everybody else thought of *them*. Why else would Mr. Zammit spend so much time making his stupid PowerPoints sing and dance if he didn't want us to think he was cool?

No, it was the way Mom was talking about Grandma Yvette. I'd seen enough clenched teeth and forced smiles between them to know that they weren't each other's biggest fans. Neither of them would be wearing a T-shirt with the other's face on it anytime soon (though that might be a good way to resolve fights, I noted for later, because how could someone stay mad at you if you were wearing a T-shirt with their giant face on it?). But both Mom and Grandma Yvette had always been very careful not to say anything bad about each other to me before. Even if it wasn't that hard to figure out what *It doesn't matter what I think about her* and *I respect her life decisions* actually meant.

"Really, her attitude toward you was written before you were even born. I don't think there's anything you could have done to change it," Mom said.

"Because she didn't like you?"

Mom didn't even flinch. "No, she doesn't particularly like me. But it's more than that—she doesn't like that Dad married me."

"What's the difference?"

"It all comes down to control," Mom said. "And power. Your grandma is desperate for everybody to do whatever she wants, and if they don't listen to her, she punishes them."

Like . . . Sarah. I'd seen this before, with her and Sarah.

Maybe Sarah was just as afraid of her as I was. Only in a different way.

"It's why she likes that doll so much," Mom said. Gus. She was talking about Gus and his real-looking butt, except she probably didn't know about his butt, because she'd never depantsed him like Sarah and I had. That had been a fun day, actually. One of the few times I'd seen Sarah giggle so hard she couldn't catch her breath. "Because it can't defy her. She can dress it up in whatever she wants and pose it however she wants and plop it down wherever she wants, and it will never, ever do something she doesn't like."

Wow. I'd never thought about it that way. "Why are you saying this now?" I asked. I was going to clarify what I meant, but it turned out my mom didn't need it. She turned on me with a fierce smile, the look I assumed an antelope would see right before the lion pounced on her.

244

Except I wasn't the antelope. Grandma Yvette was the antelope.

"That woman can come for me all she wants," Mom said. "But I won't ever let her come for you."

My mom's conviction got me through the next few days, until the third Junior Sisterhood meeting. When Aubrey and I walked into the social hall, even more kids than last time sat around the table—not just Talia, Kira, and Ellie, but three others. Plus Sarah, whose sling had been removed the day before.

"I think we're going to need another table," Sarah said with a big wide smile. A suspiciously big wide smile.

As she ordered the other kids to go drag one over, I sidled up next to her. "What are you doing here?"

She turned that big wide smile on me. I blinked. For a moment, she looked like Grandma Yvette. "It's my club, Ruby. Why wouldn't I be here?"

"It's Sarah's," I hissed. "Not yours."

She didn't respond, only nodded at the kids who'd dragged the other table over. They nudged it so that the two round tables together made an *8* shape, and arranged the chairs around it. I jumped and managed to get a seat next to Sarah, who was sitting across from Rabbi Ellen.

"Whatever you're up to, I'm going to make sure you don't wreck this," I said. For my sake. For Rabbi Ellen's. For all the other kids'.

Sarah—the dybbuk—just smiled enigmatically at me in response.

The first part of Junior Sisterhood actually went pretty well. We were continuing our discussion of the Torah portions about Joseph and his life, and everybody had a lot to say. Except Sarah, who sat slouched down in her chair, her arms crossed. Which was fine by me. Better sullen and silent than actively making a mess.

Of course, just as I thought that, someone loudly cleared their throat. I jumped in my seat. Somehow I'd missed Grandma Yvette walking in through the door behind me and over to our table. Now she stood there, her arms crossed. Even though I didn't have my phone out or anything, for a moment I felt exposed, like she was reading my texts over my shoulder.

"Sarah, I need your help in the kitchen again," she said without greeting Rabbi Ellen or any of us, really. "The temple board is meeting tonight to elect the new president, and we're shorthanded making the snacks."

Sarah's head jerked up like somebody had hit her. "Again? Even after last time?"

When she'd juggled the plates. Grandma Yvette's lips thinned at the reminder. "I know you'll behave this time," she said. "Now come."

Like last time, Sarah turned to Rabbi Ellen, and the sullen look lifted right off her face. Her eyes pleaded. She didn't even have to say anything.

I could say something. I could open my mouth and speak up for her. That might keep the dybbuk from doing something terrible.

Rabbi Ellen sighed. "Yvette, are you sure this can't wait? We're having a great discussion right now."

I opened my mouth . . . and, once again, the words just wouldn't come. I couldn't get past the idea of Grandma Yvette pinching her lips at me and saying my name in that cold, cold voice.

"This cannot wait," Grandma Yvette said flatly. "Sarah, come."

Rabbi Ellen sighed again, only this time she didn't say anything. Anything at all. Not even as Grandma towed Sarah from the room by her hand.

The discussion lost some vigor after that; it was like we were just going through the motions, but didn't really care about them. I only half paid attention, too busy worrying about Sarah and the dybbuk.

And then I heard a throat clear again. This time my head shot up to see Sarah standing at the door. Everybody turned to look at her. Usually all the eyes on her would make Sarah blush, but the dybbuk seemed to revel in them all, and she straightened up as she walked farther into the room, her eyes blazing.

"Oh, I'm glad you're done in the kitchen," Rabbi Ellen said.

"I'm not done. I said I had to go to the bathroom," Sarah said, and her voice was deadly quiet as she went on. "Rabbi Ellen. If you were one of Joseph's brothers, do you think you would have sold him into slavery the way they did? Or would you have spoken up against it?"

My stomach clenched. I couldn't blame Sarah for being annoyed at what had happened, but whatever the dybbuk had planned, I was sure it wasn't good. So before anyone could answer, I interjected, "Ha ha, very funny, Sarah! She's a jokester, that one!" Everybody was staring at me. I could feel my face heat up bright red. "Um, let's just keep going. Pay her no mind."

"No, I never want to dismiss a question," said Rabbi Ellen, frowning at me ever so slightly.

"Yeah, Ruby, why would you want to dismiss my question?" Sarah said sweetly.

Ugh.

Rabbi Ellen nodded at Sarah. "I think it's our responsibility as Jews to stand up for the unfortunate and downtrodden," she said. "What else do you think our responsibilities are?"

"You didn't answer the question." Sarah stared right at her.

I interjected again. "Yes, she did! Let's move on! I think our responsibilities are—"

"You want to know what I think?" Sarah might actually have been trying to bore holes in Rabbi Ellen's forehead with the force of her gaze. I almost expected her eyes to flash red again. "I think you totally would've sold Joseph off if you were his sister."

Some of the other kids gasped, Aubrey included. Rabbi Ellen blinked hard, like she wasn't quite sure what she'd heard. If I were her, I probably would've said something scornful, but Rabbi Ellen only blinked again and asked, "Why do you say that, Sarah?"

Sarah pressed her lips together hard. For a moment she looked like she might cry. "Because you were totally fine letting my grandma take me away to cook when I didn't want to! Twice now!"

Rabbi Ellen looked a little bit like she might cry, too.

"Sarah, I'm so sorry you feel that way—" she began, but Sarah interrupted.

"Any apology that starts that way isn't a real apology." Sarah stomped her foot that wasn't in a brace, and somehow the noise seemed to echo throughout the room. All of us around the table jumped. "You sold me out."

"Why don't we plan to talk about this in my office later?" Rabbi Ellen asked. Her eyebrows met over her nose, pointing down in a troubled *V*. "We can figure this out."

"There's nothing to figure out." Sarah tossed her hair and backed up, heading toward the door. I guess there was only so long she could pretend to be in the bathroom. "You act like you're some great trailblazer for women, but you're not at all. You can spout off about how there are a thousand right ways to be Jewish or whatever, but I didn't want to go, and you didn't stand up for me."

"Sarah, if your grandmother comes and pulls you out, I'm not *allowed* to stand up to her!" The words burst out of Rabbi Ellen's' mouth with a force that seemed to surprise even her. "Your parents and guardians have the right to pull you out of class if they want to. I think we should all sit down together and work out a—"

"That's because she wouldn't listen to you." Sarah's voice was very quiet. All the other kids leaned in to hear her, like flowers stretching toward the sun. "She would've listened to the old rabbi. Maybe because he was a man, or maybe because she liked him more. Either way . . ." She trailed off, squinting at Rabbi Ellen as if she were thinking hard.

"We'll figure this out, Sarah," Rabbi Ellen said.

"Oh, don't worry," Sarah said. "I already have."

And just like that, she walked out. I hastily excused myself to follow her, but I couldn't find her anywhere. I went back to the meeting, but couldn't focus on the rest of the discussion. Her words were busy tumbling around in my head. What had she meant?

CHAPTER TWENTY

THE WHOLE NEXT DAY I was on edge, waiting for the other shoe to drop. Sarah's other shoe, specifically. But everything seemed normal. Sarah was in school, and didn't get any detentions. We took the bus to Grandma Yvette's later and got off together, Sarah limping along on her ankle brace.

Grandma Yvette greeted us at the door. I cocked my head at her, squinting, trying to see her the way my mom had described her. *A sad, mean old woman.*

But all I saw was my grandma. And she smiled down at me as usual, so she didn't seem so sad. "Hi, my dears," she said. "Ready to help make some cakes?"

For the next hour I mixed batter, whipped frosting, and carefully inserted knives into the center of cakes to make sure they were fully cooked. Sarah disappeared somewhere in the middle, saying that she was going to the bathroom and then never coming back. I was red-faced and sweaty by the time all the cakes were cooling on the counter. Really sweaty. I was pretty sure I'd sweated into some of these cakes, actually. Hopefully their eaters wouldn't mind the extra salt. Or grossness.

"Thank you, Ruby. You've been a great help," Grandma Yvette said, beaming down at me. I tucked a damp curl behind my ear, proud of myself. "I'm going to go lie down. Why don't you go see how Sarah's doing? She's been in the bathroom for quite a while."

Sarah was not in the bathroom. I found her downstairs in the den, lying on the floor, her arms stretched out over her head. Gus sat on his usual chair, watching over her with his (literally) beady black eyes.

Curiosity got the best of me. "What are you doing?" I asked Sarah, not Gus, because Gus was doing the same thing as he always did.

The dybbuk turned Sarah's head to look at me. Her eyes glowed red for a split second, then faded back into

Sarah's usual brown. "She's fighting me hard today," the dybbuk said conversationally. "She hasn't realized yet that it's useless."

Nausea rose in my gullet. The dybbuk had said something about Sarah fighting her before, but aside from that, I hadn't thought about whether Sarah was still there, awake, while the dybbuk used her body. For some reason I'd just assumed she was . . . sleeping, or unconscious, or something.

But if Sarah was fighting . . . this was probably a good time for me to try and expel the dybbuk. No matter that it required a pious Jew, and I apparently wasn't that. And that I didn't have a *minyan*. Or prayers. Or anything else, really. Just me, Ruby Diana Taylor.

But was "just me" enough?

I rolled my shoulders back, then squared them. Whether I was enough or not, I had to try. I fixed the dybbuk with what I hoped was a fierce stare, projecting fire from my eyes. Maybe if I focused hard enough, they'd glow red like the dybbuk's.

When I spoke, I tried to project the same sense of fierceness—a dragon breathing fire. "I command you to leave Sarah's body," I said. And then in Hebrew a psalm I'd seen online that was apparently used in exorcisms during the Middle Ages: *The LORD seeks out the righteous man, but loathes the wicked one who loves injustice. He will rain down upon the wicked blazing coals and sulfur; a scorching wind shall be their lot.*

I paused. "That's you," I told the dybbuk, in case she didn't get it. "You're the wicked one."

"Thanks," the dybbuk replied. I was pretty sure she was being sarcastic.

In any case, I waved my arms in what I hoped was a mystical fashion. "Go!" I commanded. "You're wasting your time, anyway. Sarah's stronger than you are." I was starting to lose the fire and the fury, so I focused back into it. "Begone!"

I stared down the dybbuk. The dybbuk stared back at me. What was she seeing? A kid? Well, so what—I *was* a kid. Someone pious? I was pious. I was pretty sure reciting psalms in Hebrew proved that. A Jew?

Well.

My iron gaze faltered. I let my guard down for a moment. I took a step back.

The dybbuk's smile flashed. It knew. *She* knew. She knew I didn't count as a Jew, and so she didn't have to listen to me.

I opened my mouth, ready to yell at her again, but then

closed it, because what was the point? I'd failed. Not only that, I'd failed in thinking I could ever do this in the first place. I'd failed because of *what* I was, not *who* I was.

The dybbuk got up. "That was fun," she said, and then she limped up the stairs. I followed, feeling useless, like a tail on a human being.

She stopped in the kitchen, her eyes sweeping over the room. They snagged for a moment on Sarah's drawing on the fridge, then moved on. Over the table, the sink full of dishes, the cakes cooling on the counter.

The cakes.

I ran up as she took a step toward them, a wicked smile growing over her lips. "What do you think about a cake fight?" she asked me.

No. No way. Not these cakes I'd helped make. Not the one cooking-related task I'd done a good job on. But I could practically see it. The dybbuk's fists sinking into the layers of chocolate and vanilla and red velvet. The sweet cake squishing between her fingers, frosting squirting out through the cracks. Cake splattering over clean cabinets and swept floors and my shirt.

Her hands reached for the nearest cake, a layered cookies-and-cream concoction full of my sweat and tears.

No. No way.

I threw myself at Sarah. Our bodies met with a thunder-clap; she shrieked as I pushed her away. She pushed back at me, and I pushed back at her, and the first thing I had over her was that I was stronger and the second thing was that she was injured, so that meant I tackled her. She landed on her back on the kitchen floor, her eyes wide as they stared up at me.

"Is everything okay down there?" Grandma Yvette called.

I turned to yell up the stairs, "We're fine!" and when I turned back I found Sarah's eyes flashing red. I gasped. A grimace contorted her mouth.

And then the words drifted weakly from her lips. "Ruby . . . Ruby . . . It's me . . ."

Her voice sounded almost the same, but thready. And even though it was possible this was another trick from the dybbuk . . . I knew. I knew it was Sarah. The real Sarah.

This being Sarah, she proved it to me anyway. "Ask me . . . a question . . ."

I jumped off her and sat cross-legged at her side so that I could look right in her face. And know if the dybbuk came back. Where was it now? Probably the same place where Sarah was when the dybbuk was in her head—pushed underneath, or shoved under a blanket. "What's my favorite thing to cook?"

A smile danced faintly over her lips. "Nothing. You hate . . . cooking."

That proved it twice over, then. "Sarah," I said, because it felt good to say her name after all this time. "Did we do it? Is it gone?"

The smile flickered and died. "No. I just pushed it back . . . for a little while."

"Oh."

"Thank you . . . for trying. I didn't know . . . you cared."

"Of course I care." I pushed down the guilt I felt at the words the dybbuk had told me before. That Sarah had been sad. That she'd missed me.

"Thank . . . you."

For some reason, tears stung the backs of my eyes. "I'm sorry. That I couldn't do more." I wanted to go on and tell her that it wasn't my fault, that I couldn't help it that my mom wasn't Jewish, but the words stuck in my throat.

"It's . . . okay," Sarah said. She gasped in a breath, like it hurt to speak. Guilt hammered me again, because she wasn't even blaming me for unleashing this thing into her in the first place. "It's not . . . your fault."

It kind of *was* my fault, though. I'd started the fight that led to me knocking the dybbuk box over.

I am so sick of you. Of how perfect you are all the time. I'm always being compared to you, you know that? And I'm always coming up short. That's why Grandma Yvette likes you more than me. I'm so sick of it, and I'm so sick of you.

The sound of my own words in my head made me wither in shame. I'd been really mean. Uncalled-for mean. Realizing that made me feel kind of sick. A heavy sort of sick, like you get before you throw up.

But something was still unresolved. "What about the Incident?" I asked. No recognition lit up her eyes. Of course. The Incident wasn't capitalized in *her* head. To her, it would just be another day. So I explained how I'd overheard Grandma Yvette telling her I didn't count as a Jew, how she'd gone right along with it, said that being with them might be "good for me." How it had hurt me.

She let her breath out in a long, low whoosh. "I didn't know . . . you were there."

I didn't respond, because it shouldn't matter whether I was there to hear it or not. It was wrong.

"I should have . . . said something . . . to Grandma," Sarah said. "I knew . . . she was wrong. But . . . I was afraid. I didn't want . . . her to . . . get mad at me."

And . . . I knew how she felt. I, too, had been afraid to speak up to Grandma Yvette at Junior Sisterhood both times Sarah got pulled away because I didn't want that stern glare of disapproval turned on me.

But before I could say anything, Sarah continued. "She was . . . wrong. I . . . knew that. I . . . *know* that. You're Jewish. We're both . . . Jewish. Totally Jewish. I said the . . . 'good for you' thing . . . because I thought that might . . . change her mind. Not because . . . I believed it."

I understood. Because I couldn't stand up to Grandma Yvette myself, and because I knew how it felt to say things to her to try to make her approve. And it did feel good to hear Sarah explicitly say that I was as Jewish as she was. I mean, Sarah knew everything, so if she was saying it, it had to be true. "I get it. And . . . I'm really sorry for the things I said to you in the basement," I said, and I was totally sincere, and a little bit of that heaviness inside me lightened. "I shouldn't have been so mean."

"I tried . . . with you. I invited you for . . . ice cream . . . when Grandma took me for my report card," Sarah grunted, and her body shook a little bit, like she was having a seizure. But she relaxed without her eyes glowing red, which I thought meant it was still her in there. At least for now.

"Wait . . . you did?" I thought back to that day outside

Hebrew school after Sarah had started Junior Sisterhood. I'd assumed that Sarah was telling me about the ice cream to rub in the fact that I didn't get any. So much so that I'd stopped listening to what she was saying next. She was right. She'd been inviting me to come with her, and I'd shoved her aside. "I . . . maybe I shouldn't have assumed."

Sarah forced out, "But you meant it . . . what you said. And you . . . were right."

She went on before I could say anything more. "Grandma is . . . not as nice to you. Because . . . your mom isn't Jewish. And it's not . . . right. I know . . . that. But . . . I took it all . . . anyway."

"It's not your fault," I told her, and as those words came out of my mouth, they shifted something inside me, something I should have known all along. It really wasn't Sarah's fault that Grandma Yvette treated the two of us the way she did. The Incident wasn't her fault. It wasn't my fault, either.

It was all on Grandma Yvette.

And if there was anything I'd learned through all of this, it was that Sarah was a victim, too. Always having to do what Grandma Yvette expected of her, even if it wasn't what she wanted. Was it better to have no expectations, or too many?

Sarah struggled to take a breath. "I thought maybe if . . . I was less perfect for a while . . . you would like me more. That we would be . . . best friends again." Then sighed it all out. "For a little bit . . . I thought it might be . . . good to have the . . . dybbuk here . . . that it would help . . . with you."

A tender lump swelled in the back of my throat. It meant tears. I looked up so that they would just pool in my eyes and not slip embarrassingly down my face. "With me?"

"Not just . . . with you." Sarah's voice was a little froggy, too. "You know . . . I don't have many friends. They think . . . the same as you do. Call me . . . teacher's pet. Call me . . . little miss perfect. So I thought . . . I needed some help to . . ." She trailed off, then started again. "Win you back . . . we could be . . . the way we used to . . ."

But . . . even if I was wrong, that wasn't what I wanted. Not really. "I don't think we *can* go back to the way we used to be," I said honestly. Guilt pricked me again as Sarah's face fell. "I mean, I want to be friends. With you. I think we can do that. But we were always together! I want to have other friends, too."

"Other . . . friends?"

The words tumbled out of me in a rush, like they'd

been waiting to come out for a long time. "We'll always have each other. There's so much history we have in common. And we do have fun, sometimes." It was true. "But we also just have a lot of different interests. So I can be friends with you and we can hang out sometimes and talk about things, and then I can be friends with Aubrey and we can hang out and do other things. And you can have me, as usual, but maybe also a friend who likes the same things you like. Like studying and debating and drawing." A face popped into my head. "Like Jamilah from my science class, actually. Do you know her? I think you guys would actually get along really well."

"Maybe . . ."

She was hurting. I'd been selfish. And mean. I closed my eyes. Why hadn't I just talked to her about this before? "Sarah . . ." I opened my eyes and looked back at my cousin, ready to give her a heartfelt apology . . .

. . . and found a ghoulish smile on her face, her eyes shining bright red.

"Ahhh!" I jumped in place, falling backward. You'd think I would've learned not to do that by now. I'd have a bruise on my tailbone tomorrow.

Sarah—the dybbuk—sat up, yawning and stretching. "Well, that was quite enough of that, don't you think?

What a drip." It lowered Sarah's voice and said, mockingly, "I *thought* maybe *if* I *could* be *a* little *more* like *youuuuu* . . ."

My fists clenched by my sides. "Shut up."

"What was that?" The voice came from the top of the stairs where the bedrooms were. I looked up to see Grandma Yvette squinting down at me. Of course. *That's* the part she would overhear, because the universe hates me.

"Not only did you wake me up with all this commotion, now you're telling your cousin to 'shut up,'" Grandma Yvette said. "Apologize right now, Ruby. You know I won't tolerate that sort of language in my home."

My jaw clenched along with my fists. Despite everything, despite what I'd just realized . . . I still wanted Grandma Yvette to smile at me, not just Sarah. "Sorry," I bit out, turning back toward Sarah so I could glare at the dybbuk without Grandma Yvette seeing.

"Good," Grandma Yvette said. "You're fortunate that Sarah is so kind and forgiving, Ruby."

Ugh.

I had to get the dybbuk out of Sarah. And while Sarah saying I was just as Jewish as her made me feel better, I didn't think it was enough. Not to face the dybbuk.

CHAPTER
TWENTY-ONE

AUBREY WAS PRACTICALLY BOUNCING IN her seat the next day at Hebrew school. She spent the whole time sketching out costume ideas for her stint as the singing feather duster and asking for my opinions. I had no idea what Mrs. Rosen was trying to teach us, but Aubrey and I did figure out a costume on our way down the stairs at the end of the day. Sarah had already run off the second she could, so I didn't have to watch out for her. "Definitely feathers," she said. "Just so many feathers. Like, more feathers than you've ever seen in your entire life."

"That's a lot of feathers." I glanced down the admin-istration hallway and noticed a spill of light hitting the carpet. From the rabbi's office. Rabbi Ellen burning the midnight oil? Or, six-thirty oil? We didn't have a Junior Sisterhood meeting today. I would assume she'd want to beat it before any of the old people could corner her and ask her boring questions.

"Soooo many! And they'll all be glued to me! I'll be the most glamorous feather duster the world has ever seen!"

As a rabbi, she was one of the people who should theoretically know the most about Judaism. Would she have more information on how to get rid of a dybbuk than my assorted Google searches?

I paused at the hallway door. "Let's do some final sketches of your costume this weekend," I told Aubrey. "And I want to see your *qipao*, too!"

"Yes!" She leaned in and gave me a spontaneous hug. I hugged her tightly back. I felt warm, and not just because of the hug. Because I was really happy with how our friendship was working out. This moment of talking about costumes and enthusing about making one was something so unlike I'd ever had before with Sarah. But that didn't make it better or worse. Just different.

Aubrey checked her phone. "My mom's waiting outside. See you tomorrow!"

She dashed out the door, leaving me there. I cracked open the hallway door, trying to get up the nerve to walk toward that pool of light.

A shadow. I stepped back before Rabbi Ellen could see me . . . and then realized that the shadow had looked awfully small to be a grown woman. Like, it looked about the size of a twelve-year-old girl.

My hackles raised. The hair stood up on the back of my neck.

I didn't need nerve to walk down that hallway now. I was practically running, afraid what I'd see when I got there.

Sarah turned as soon as I stepped through the doorway, almost like she was expecting me. Then she sighed heavily, like she definitely was not. "Oh. It's you."

I'd never been in the rabbi's office before now. Back when the rabbi had been Rabbi Jacob—an old man with a beard who always smelled like steamed broccoli—I'd pictured the office as a small, dark, cramped space, full of books and menorahs and overcooked green vegetables.

Rabbi Ellen's space was full of light. Even though there was only one window and that window was dark with night, lamps rested atop the desk and the bookshelf and the windowsill and the file cabinet near the door, shining green and pink and blue and white through stained glass shades. They made me think of the stained glass windows in the temple sanctuary.

So many things for the dybbuk to smash and destroy. Sarah was standing in front of Rabbi Ellen's bookshelf, face tilted up as if she was reading all the titles. Maybe that was it. Maybe she was just here for a little mental enrichment.

And then I saw the match in her hand, and my breath froze in my throat.

"So much kindling," Sarah said in a conversational way. "Old, dry books. They'll be ablaze before you can even blink. Once the fire's that big, it'll tear through the rest of the building like it's made out of toothpicks."

"Put the match down," I said.

"I don't think I will." Sarah's smile widened. "Rabbi Ellen needs to be taught a lesson. She's not the good person she pretends to be, not after she did nothing to help Sarah."

The dybbuk went to strike the match. I wouldn't have time to tackle her. Time seemed to slow as my eyes darted frantically around the room, landing on a stack of papers, a lamp, a stapler . . .

I grabbed the stapler and I threw. It sailed in an arc through the air, tumbling end over end . . . and striking her hard on the shoulder of her uninjured arm. She cried out, her body jerking. Her fingers burst open. The unlit match fell to the floor, disappearing in a stack of books.

I started to breathe a little easier. Even as Sarah glared at me, her shoulders hunching forward. "How dare you," she said. "Wait until I—" Her eyes cleared. Her shoulders relaxed. "Rabbi Ellen! Ruby just threw a stapler at me!" She clutched her shoulder, wincing in pain. "I was just waiting here to talk to you, and she started attacking me!"

I girded myself to protest, to explain the truth but not *too* much of the truth, and then I realized that Rabbi Ellen was frowning like she didn't believe her.

Well, that was a nice change. Though I guess not surprising, considering how Sarah had behaved toward her lately. And also just behaved in general.

"I stepped outside to talk to a parent in the parking lot. Your parents are waiting, Sarah," she said. "You'd better head out."

Sarah's eyes narrowed. She wrinkled her nose.

She stomped out without another word.

I still couldn't avoid the urge to explain myself. "I did throw the stapler, but only because she was going to—"

"Ruby. Why don't you sit down?" Rabbi Ellen said.

"Sit down?" I asked.

"I was hoping I'd see you, actually. We have something to talk about."

She sat down behind her desk. Her chair squeaked. I took one of the plush chairs facing her. From this angle, I could see all of the family photos on her desk, the frames shining against all the light. There was a younger Rabbi Ellen, her hair not silver but brown, smiling wide in a white dress next to a man in a tuxedo. The man had a mustache. Another photo showed Rabbi Ellen, her hair brown again, holding a baby, next to another photo of her holding another baby, only her hair was silver this time. I guess it could have been the same baby, because babies all look the same, except for the hair.

"I went gray overnight," she told me, seeing me looking again. "One day in my forties. It felt like I went to bed with brown hair and woke up with gray."

I cocked my head. Her hair seemed to glitter against the light just like those shiny frames. "I like it. I think it's more silver than gray."

"You know?" She leaned over her desk, like she was going to tell me a secret. "I like it, too."

Then she leaned back, and it was like I could feel something in the air shift. "Ruby, I've been thinking about the night of your grandmother's Chanukah party." She looked at me thoughtfully, just as she had the night of the Chanukah party, and something inside me shriveled up, remembering how I'd felt that awful night.

I had to say something before she could. "About the Chanukah party," I said, and her mouth opened, but I plowed ahead anyway. "I wasn't trying to steal the Shabbat candles. I wouldn't do that. At least not in front of everybody." No, that made me look bad. "I mean, I wouldn't do it at all, but *especially* not in front of everybody." I sighed. I still didn't think that made me look great, but I had to move on. "Sarah's been acting kind of . . . weird, lately, as you've seen, and I was worried she'd try and destroy the candles."

"I've seen," Rabbi Ellen said gently. "For what it's worth, I wouldn't have blamed you for trying to grab them."

I blinked. "What?" A rabbi couldn't be advocating theft, right? That would be like Mr. Zammit telling us to go ahead and cheat on our next test because we'd never use any of it in real life. Which he would never do. He was always going on and on about how we would definitely need to know how the water cycle worked if we were going to make it in the real world.

Rabbi Ellen sighed. "I've given a lot of thought to what

271

Sarah said to me in our last Junior Sisterhood meeting. But not just how it applied to Sarah—how it applied to you." *Me?* "I won't talk to you about Sarah—that's for me and Sarah and her parents. But I regret not speaking up for you at the party, Ruby. And I apologize for that. Obviously your grandmother has the right to give whatever gifts to whatever people she wants, but she was wrong to say that you're not Jewish. Because you are."

I assumed she meant that to be inspirational, but all I heard were empty words. I asked her, "Are both your parents Jewish?"

She hesitated for a moment, then nodded. I scoffed for a moment before I realized what I was doing. I couldn't scoff at a *rabbi*!

No matter how much she was just trying to make me feel better. "You wouldn't get it, then," I said. "Nobody's ever questioned whether you have the right to be here."

I almost couldn't believe what happened next—she scoffed back! At me! Scoffed!

She must have seen how wide my eyes got, because she doubled over with a hearty belly laugh. "I'm sorry, my dear," she said. She reached up and wiped at the corners of her eyes. "I'm not laughing at you, I promise. It's just . . . the idea that nobody's ever questioned my right to be here . . ."

She leaned over her desk again, her face going serious. "Things are better than they used to be, there's no question about that. But there are a whole lot of people out there—in this synagogue, even!—who were definitely not ready for a female rabbi."

Oh. That was right. I remembered how, when she'd first spoken to our class, she'd told us about the people who questioned her right to be on the bima. Who assumed her husband was the rabbi. Who thought she belonged maybe not at home, but anywhere else. And Grandma Yvette had basically said the same thing.

"How did you convince them that you deserved to be here?" I asked her. I mean, she had to have changed their minds, just like I'd change Grandma Yvette's mind, and then I'd be a real Jew who could expel the dybbuk.

She shook her head, as if she could read my mind. "I didn't," she said. "There are always going to be people who won't accept me. Who won't accept you. But that doesn't mean *you're* the one who isn't right."

But . . . all of the laws. All of the ancient rabbis.

"There is no explicit line in the Torah that says Judaism

is passed down only through the mother," Rabbi Ellen said. "Generations of rabbis and sages have deduced it from stories in the text, and yes, it's common custom, but no law tells us that you can only be Jewish if your mother is Jewish. Just as there's no explicit command from Hashem that women cannot be rabbis—just the interpretation of the laws of men over thousands of years. Why, did you know when the first female rabbi lived?"

I had no idea, so I picked a random year from a long time ago. "1980?"

She shook her head. "The early sixteen hundreds. Her name was Asenath Barzani, and she lived in Iraq."

Okay, that was a *really* long time ago. But as interesting as it was, I was more interested in how this all applied to me. "You really think . . ." I trailed off, because I didn't really know what I was trying to ask her. I didn't want to make it seem like I was desperate or something, asking for her opinion.

"Let me ask you what *you* think," Rabbi Ellen said. That wasn't an answer to my question, but okay. "Do you think I deserve to be up on that bima?"

"Of course." I didn't even have to think about it. "You went to rabbinical school, didn't you? And you're good at what you do." I felt safe saying that, just from the way she was talking to me.

"Thank you, Ruby. I am. Because I don't need ancient scholars to tell me what I believe, I know what I know," she said. "Just as I know you're Jewish. Full stop."

Maybe it was all the lamps around me, but I was starting to feel kind of a glow on the inside. Like, inside my ribs.

It could have been indigestion, I guess. "But what about the thousands and thousands of years of tradition?" I asked.

Rabbi Ellen raised an eyebrow. "Just because it's the way it's been done for thousands and thousands of years," she said, "doesn't make it right."

I let the full force of those words hit me, but they didn't make me heavier. It was like they fanned the glow inside me, made it brighter. Lighter. It was like the light of a pair of Shabbat candles, or a Chanukah menorah, shining their candles in the dark night. Letting me see all the things I couldn't see before.

Like the fact that I'd been focusing too hard on what Grandma Yvette had been saying and not listening to anyone else. To the light inside me that shined the truth from my eyes, my ears, my mouth. Like I'd been focusing too hard on being annoyed at whatever Sarah did, her grades and her hair and her behavior, rather than trying to change my own. Like I was finally understanding what Rabbi Ellen had said about her mother's dry mandelbrot, and that even if some people loved mandelbrot and wanted to eat them for every holiday and that was okay, that didn't mean that *everybody* had to eat and like mandelbrot.

I *was* a Jew. I *am* a Jew. Grandma Yvette could think whatever she wanted, just like those people who thought a woman shouldn't be a rabbi could think whatever they wanted. That was their right. But Rabbi Ellen was still our rabbi, and I was still a Jew. And as long as I knew that, I could take out that dybbuk.

I opened my mouth, half-expecting to vomit up a sunbeam. That would've been cool, if anatomically impossible. What came out instead was, "Thank you, Rabbi Ellen."

"You don't need to thank me," Rabbi Ellen said, and smiled. "I was only telling you something you already knew."

CHAPTER TWENTY-TWO

I SHOWED UP AT GRANDMA Yvette's house after school the next day full of fire and fury. I was ready to burn things. At least metaphorically. Probably not literally. I didn't want to be as bad as the dybbuk. Or get arrested for arson.

I marched up the front steps and threw open the door. Grandma Yvette was standing there, her arm reaching out to open the door herself. Her lips parted in surprise. "Oh, hello, Ruby," she said.

I puffed my chest out, full of things I wanted to say. Or to yell, really. *You're wrong. Like, so wrong. You're mean and unhappy and you don't know everything. It's not right of you to pit me and Sarah against each other the way you've done our whole lives, because even if part of the blame is mine, part of it is yours, too.*

What I actually said was, "Hi, Grandma," and I closed my eyes as she kissed me on the forehead. Her lips felt like a brush of paper. The smell of smoke drifted over me.

I wasn't that brave. Because even if I knew I was right, I still didn't think I could handle the displeased down-turn of her lips, directed at me. Which made me feel even more for Sarah during the Incident, made me understand her more.

I took a deep breath. Since Sarah hadn't been on the bus, I asked, "Is Sarah already here?"

Grandma Yvette shook her head. Her silver hair swung neatly from side to side. "Sarah's not feeling well, unfor-tunately," she said. "She's at home. So it's just you and me today."

Normally I'd be happy to hear that. Excited, even. But today the news filled me with disappointment. I'd been ready to get rid of the dybbuk today. All fired up. What if that fire went out?

I tried to stay fiery as we stirred pots and kneaded dough, but it was hard to stoke a flame when you were smelling notes of chocolate and raspberry in the air. By the time Grandma Yvette asked me to go down to the basement and fetch her some more powdered sugar from the pantry, I was slumped over with gloominess again.

I paused before going down into the basement. From here, I locked eyes with Gus sitting in his usual chair in the den. His cloth arms flopped comfortably over the armrests; his peach-fabric stomach poked through his blue plaid shirt. "I wish I had your life, Gus. You have everything so easy," I said, then reconsidered. "Though I guess you don't really have a life at all."

Plus, everything he had came from Grandma Yvette. His shirts, which used to be Grandpa Joel's. His name.

His name.

Something clicked in my head.

"Ruby, where's that powdered sugar? I have to ice these cakes when they cool!" Grandma Yvette yelled from the kitchen. She started coughing, saving me from having to reply as I rushed down the basement stairs. I didn't go toward the pantry. I went toward the back, toward the dybbuk box.

I hadn't been down here since Sarah and I—okay, I—accidentally opened it, but it was still sitting where we'd left it, back near the basement fridge. Some dust had even settled on the lid. I knelt down before it and, not hesitating at all, flipped it open. I'd already loosed the dybbuk. What worse could I do?

Inside rested the items I'd seen the first time we opened the box: the small paper card covered in writing, the scrap of red fabric, and the yellowed white handkerchief with the rusty brown stain on it. I examined the card first, since writing would seem to be the best source of information, but the letters were not in English—the letters were Hebrew, which meant the language was probably either Hebrew or Yiddish, neither of which I understood well enough to figure out what it said. The scrap of red cloth led to nothing, either. It was rough, more like canvas than silk, and faded with age, but that was about all I learned from it.

That left the handkerchief, the one with the creepily bloodlike stain on it. I pulled it out between two fingers and hung it in front of my face, squinting. The bloodstain—because that was what it had to be, right?—was in the approximate shape of Texas, but that wasn't helpful. I wondered what the blood had come from. It could've come from the death of the girl who'd become the dybbuk, of course, or it could've been from a nosebleed, which made sense in regards to a handkerchief, or—

There. Writing. Embroidered in neat black thread,

letters marched across the bottom of the handkerchief. I held my breath as I brought it closer to my face to read it. I wasn't sure why. It wasn't like there were death particles on it still. And even if there were, it wasn't like death was contagious. Especially if the dybbuk-lady had died in some way that involved bleeding.

The letters were familiar! Hurrah! It took me some time to parse out the cramped, spidery black threads, but it was only a few minutes before I had a name. *Chana-Lotte.*

The name of the dybbuk? One of my online sources had said that you needed the name of something to command it. Maybe now that I knew I was a pious Jew and that I had the dybbuk's name . . .

. . . maybe now I could save Sarah.

But what to do with the dybbuk? I took a look at the paper again, then grabbed my phone. Google Translate to the rescue. Fifteen minutes of squinting and speaking later, I'd pieced together roughly what the paper said. It was a record of the people, Grandma Yvette's ancestors, who had gotten the dybbuk in the box in the first place. Apparently they'd exorcised the dybbuk from a person and trapped it in this box. That could be done, they said. And it didn't have to be a box . . .

I wondered what would happen if a dybbuk was

trapped in the body of an animal. Like a dog. Would the dog be able to talk? I could never test it out on an innocent dog, but the idea was intriguing.

My feet pounded back up the stairs, the handkerchief clutched tight in my sweaty hand. I blew past Gus without so much as a wave. Up another flight of stairs, and then I skidded to a stop in front of Grandma Yvette, panting too hard to speak.

"Where's the sugar?" Grandma Yvette asked.

Right. The sugar.

Oh well. I rolled my shoulders back, clearing my throat. "Do you know who Chana-Lotte is?" I brandished the handkerchief before me like a detective flourishing the final clue on a case, the one that would send the suspect to jail.

Grandma Yvette leaned in, squinting as hard as I did. I'd always found it kind of impressive that she was ancient years old and didn't need glasses the way both my parents did. "Where did you get this?"

Everything was already so bad, it couldn't get worse. Still, it was hard to get the words out. Despite everything, despite all I'd learned and all I knew about myself, I wanted her approval still. Craved it, like it was chocolate sitting on the counter, to show me that I was worth it. I just wanted to eat it. Even if it might be poisoned.

I took a deep breath. Then told her, "The dybbuk box."

She gasped. "What?"

"It was an accident," I started with, but it didn't make her look any happier. "I tripped over it and it flew open." I couldn't tell her about the dybbuk. She wouldn't believe me. Or worse: She'd blame me for infecting her precious perfect Sarah. "I found this inside. Do you know who it is?"

I waited for her to shake her head. To tell me I was a disappointment.

Instead, she sighed. "Of course I know of Chana-Lotte," she said. "My grandmother told me stories of her to make sure I behaved myself."

"What happened?" I said impatiently.

Grandma Yvette sighed again. "It's not a pretty story. Are you sure you don't want to wait until you're older?"

Wait until I'm older! If I waited until I was any older, Sarah would have burned down the entire town. "I'm old enough."

"If you say so. It is a disturbing story. I had nightmares about it for weeks as a kid. It made me realize that I had to listen to my elders, or I might end up like her." She cocked her head and looked somewhere over my shoulder. Though from the distant expression in her eyes, I suspected that she was looking more into the past. "This was in my grandmother's day. You know, life was very hard for Jews in the old country. The gentiles—non-Jews—didn't want us there, and they weren't shy about showing it." She leaned onto the counter, setting her chin in her palm and gazing steadily at me. "There's antisemitism in America right now, but nothing compared to what we used to face. We used to have to hide in our homes on Christian holidays to protect ourselves from the gangs of gentiles out looking to beat or burn or spit on us."

By saying "we," I knew she wasn't talking specifically about herself, because she'd been born here, like me. She was talking about all of us, Jews through history, because we were one people. I wasn't sure if she was including "me" in the "we," but she didn't have to. I knew I belonged there.

"But Chana-Lotte was determined to make things more difficult for herself." Grandma Yvette frowned. "She was only a few years older than you, and she was insistent that she wanted more than the life that had been prescribed for her, which was a perfectly fine life, if you asked me: marriage; children; keeping a home. But she wanted to study, and travel, and work beside the men."

That didn't sound so terrible, if you asked *me*. Also, the

dybbuk had been a few years older than me? She hadn't seemed it. If anything, she seemed younger. Maybe a hundred years trapped in a box did that to you.

"Some Jewish women did do that back then, but not those in Chana-Lotte's community. She went to the wife of the rabbi and told her all that she wanted, and all that she didn't want. Chana-Lotte said that she wished she could be a rabbi herself. The rabbi's wife nodded along and said that she'd speak up for Chana-Lotte with her husband, that she would help her, but of course she didn't mean it. Obviously, she thought Chana-Lotte was touched in the head. So once the girl left, the rabbi's wife went right to Chana-Lotte's parents and told them everything she had told her."

What a betrayal. No wonder the dybbuk had been so angry at Rabbi Ellen for not standing up for her.

"Chana-Lotte's father immediately sent her away to be married to an old man, a man with a temper, the only one who would take her, given all these whispers of disobedience," Grandma Yvette said. "From what I understand, her marriage was short and angry, and it wasn't long before Chana-Lotte died in a fire." She paused, and her next words were heavy. "A fire she'd set herself."

As furious as I was with the dybbuk for what she was

doing to Sarah, I couldn't help but feel sorry for her. If she'd been born today, her life would've been so different.

Grandma Yvette went on. "And not long after they got word of her death, my bubbe, who was only a young child, started acting strange and rebelling against her family. When she got into trouble, she claimed she was possessed by the spirit of Chana-Lotte."

I was starting to feel faint. It took me a second to realize that I'd been holding my breath. When I sucked in a great gasp of air, it all went straight to my head, which didn't help with the dizziness. "But how did her dybbuk get in the box?" The dybbuk must have gone into her bubbe, and then someone had expelled it and trapped it in the box. Just like on the piece of paper.

Grandma Yvette looked at me sternly. "Dybbuks aren't real. You know that."

So what she was saying was that she didn't know. When I expelled the dybbuk from Sarah, should I put it back in the box? That was dangerous. As I'd learned all too well, boxes could be opened.

"Thanks for telling me all of this," I said.

"You're welcome, Ruby," she said. "I hope you'll learn from the story of Chana-Lotte, the way I did." Her eyes grew distant for a moment, like she was looking right through the walls of the house into the horizon. "I worry about you and Sarah. That you'll end up like her."

"But things are different now than they were back then," I said, and my heart leapt. Maybe I could change her mind. "You know, Rabbi Ellen says that traditions aren't always right for everybody. And that there are a thousand right ways to be a Jew and a thousand right ways to be a girl."

No more distance. Grandma Yvette's eyes laser-focused on me, and in them was fire. "I will not hear anything about that woman. I've had quite enough of her input, thank you very much."

Or maybe I couldn't change her mind. Maybe it would never change. Which meant I'd better focus on the dybbuk, on what I *could* change.

"Now, where's that sugar?"

I barely heard her. My mind was racing. Because now I knew the dybbuk's name. I knew I was a Jew no matter what Grandma Yvette thought. I just had to figure out somewhere to put the dybbuk, and . . . I could get rid of her. "Grandma," I said. "I have to see Sarah. It's really important."

She studied me for a moment, then sighed. "I suppose we could bring her some chicken noodle soup to help her feel better. That's very thoughtful of you, Ruby."

"That's me. Very thoughtful." That wasn't even sarcastic. I was still trying. Why? *Why, Ruby? Why are you doing this when you know it's never going to work out in your favor?*

Grandma Yvette said, "I'll just give Aunt Naomi a call and make sure it's okay."

I stood still as she dialed on her ancient house phone and put it to her ear. "Hello, Naomi? Oh, Ezra!" Her voice immediately warmed when she realized it was my uncle on the other end. It was like stepping from the frigid air-conditioning of a doctor's office into a beautiful summer day in the parking lot. "Hello, darling. Have you eaten yet today? What have you eaten? Tell your mother."

Weird—I didn't think I'd ever heard Grandma Yvette ask my dad about what he'd eaten, even though he was her other son. And come to think of it, I wasn't sure if I'd ever heard her use that tone of voice with him before.

"It sounds like you need more green vegetables," Grandma Yvette was saying. "I'll whip up that spinach salad you like with the pecans and cranberries for when Ruby and I bring Sarah some chicken soup." She paused. "What?" She blinked, shifted the phone receiver to her other ear, then blinked again. "No, she's not." Another pause. "She told you she was coming here on the bus? She told me she was sick and would be going right home!"

My heart was hammering by the time Grandma Yvette slammed the phone down on its receiver, her face grim.

Sarah—the dybbuk—had lied. She'd told her dad she'd be here and Grandma Yvette that she'd be at home, so that she could go off . . . where? The dybbuk knew I was onto her and that it was only a matter of time before I figured out how to oust her. If I were the dybbuk, this Chana-Lotte, I would plan to do something big now.

"I simply don't understand what's going on in that girl's mind lately," Grandma Yvette fretted. I could have tried to comfort her, but instead I tuned her out.

What could the dybbuk be up to? Images whirled through my mind: the purple stain on Sarah's glove after she'd pulled that fire alarm; the dybbuk's eyes glowing red on the ground outside Rabbi Ellen's house; the match in her hand in Rabbi Ellen's office; the somber look in Grandma Yvette's eyes as she recounted the story of the fire.

The fire.

Maybe the dybbuk's point *hadn't* been to pull the fire alarm. Sarah had shown that she could push off the dybbuk's control for a short period of time. And the dybbuk had shown herself as liking fire. Could the dybbuk have tried to light the school on fire . . . and Sarah fought back for a moment, pulling the fire alarm to warn everyone? And then she'd tried to burn down the temple. The temple would be closed now, but . . .

The images whirled again, then clicked together. Like a puzzle. I finally had all the pieces . . . even if my stomach churned unpleasantly at the picture it revealed.

I swallowed hard. "I know where Sarah is," I croaked out, "and we have to find her right away."

CHAPTER TWENTY-THREE

THE SUN WAS SINKING BEHIND the trees, casting a shadow over the whole world, when we pulled into my neighborhood. This was no pretty pink and orange sunset that people would come out specifically to snap a photo of and post it on their feeds with heart-eye emojis. No, this sunset was all black and blue, like a bruise.

"You think Sarah's at your house?" Grandma Yvette's knuckles were white as she gripped the steering wheel. Maybe it was the seriousness in my voice when I told her I knew where Sarah was, but she hadn't even questioned me until now. I kind of liked that, as much as I didn't like the situation. It made me feel like an adult.

"Not at my house," I said. "A different house. It's a big neighborhood. I'll tell you where to turn."

I hoped I'd know. Getting here in a car, on the street, was different than darting here through the woods in the middle of the night. Still, I thought I'd recognize the house.

I glanced over my shoulder and searched through the back window in case maybe I'd missed it. Nothing. Though my eyes did catch Gus's in the back seat. He stared at me glassily, completely missing the urgency of the situation.

Grandma Yvette had balked when I told her we had to bring him with us. "Why in the world do we need to bring a doll?" But she only gave me a jerky nod when I told her I needed him to help talk Sarah down from whatever she was doing, because Sarah and Gus had a special bond. Which was kind of weird, but could be dealt with after Sarah had her own body back.

Grandma Yvette *had* insisted on buckling Gus in. "It's not about his safety," she said sternly, reaching over him for the clasp. "In case we get into an accident, it could be dangerous to have him flying around everywhere. It's about *our* safety."

But I saw the way she patted his belly beneath Grandpa Joel's blue plaid shirt as she stepped back.

I turned away to focus on the neighborhood, and just in time. "Here." I pointed at the street corner. Grandma Yvette's car slid to a stop along the curb. She went to unbuckle, but I touched her shoulder. "You have to stay in the car."

"Excuse me?" She reached again for her seat belt, but I pushed her back more insistently.

"It can only be me out there," I said. She stayed still this time, so I backed off. "I'm the only one who can talk to Sarah when she's like this. If she sees you there . . . I don't know, she might melt down. I have to talk to her by myself."

Grandma Yvette sighed. "Okay," she said, but her eyes followed me warily as I circled around to the back of the car to get Gus. "Though if you're not back in fifteen minutes, I'm coming to get you."

"A half hour," I said.

She only tightened her lips at me. If she did anything else, I didn't see it, because I was busy unbuckling Gus and dragging him from the back seat. I almost dropped him as I tried to drape him over my shoulder. He was big, but sometimes I forgot how heavy he was. Maybe there was something inside him other than fluff. Like rocks.

Either way, I managed to drag him down the sidewalk, his bare cloth feet scraping against the concrete. I should have put some shoes on him or something. Oh well. Too late now. He'd just have to deal.

I'd specifically asked Grandma Yvette to park down the street so she wouldn't see what house I was visiting. It was fully dark, the sky a ghostly purple, by the time I reached Rabbi Ellen's house.

Its windows were dark and the front door was closed. Both of which were a relief, because I'd rather not have to explain to Rabbi Ellen and/or her family why I was outside of her house at night dragging a giant doll behind me. And Gus *was* dragging, because I'd given up struggling to hold him up. His whole backside was going to be covered in dirt. Maybe Grandma Yvette could throw him in the washing machine with his clothes.

I lugged him all the way around the side of the house. No Sarah. Maybe I was wrong. Maybe she wasn't here after all.

And then I noticed the back door yawning open. I crept toward it, all my muscles tensing, and stepped inside Rabbi Ellen's house. Should I call inside, in case Rabbi Ellen was actually home? Or—

Sarah's shadow caught my eye: It seemed extra-long and extra-dark, her fingers stretching into sharp claws and her neck into something grotesquely long. Maybe the shadow looked so dark because it was so dark inside this room, some kind of study, with a desk on one side and shelves of bookcases against the walls. Or maybe it was because I was scared. I itched to flip on the light, but I didn't want to signal to anyone outside the house we were here.

I dropped Gus instead. He landed with a thump on the carpet. The dybbuk's head jerked up. She grinned at me, and the smile stretched over her face like an oil slick, something that on its surface looked pretty (rainbows!) but was very, very wrong. "Hello, Ruby," she said. "I'm glad you're here."

"I know who you are," I said. I took a step toward her. She didn't move, only watched me with that eerie grimace. "You tried to burn the school down. But why? Didn't you want an education?"

"You don't know anything." The dybbuk scoffed. "It had nothing to do with her education. She could get an education anywhere, far away from this place. It had to do with all those jerks in the school, the ones who made fun of her or looked through her like she wasn't even there." Hurt flitted over her features for a moment before twisting back into anger. "If only she hadn't fought me off long enough to pull the alarm, we never would've had to see them again."

I'd been right, then. Again, no satisfaction. I took another step toward her. What was the dybbuk doing in here? It was too dark to see much. I'd have to get closer. I braved one more step. "And you attacked Rabbi Ellen's offices because of how the rabbi's wife way back when betrayed you."

Sarah shrugged. "I only wish the rabbi's wife was still alive so I could get revenge on her, too. But this will have to do. For Sarah's sake."

Acid rose in my throat. "You . . . you *really suck*," I told her. Okay, that was a terrible insult, but I was too frazzled to come up with anything better. "Don't you get that you're not helping Sarah? You're *hurting* her!"

Uncertainty flickered in the dybbuk's eyes. For a moment she didn't look like a monster at all. Just like a small, scared child.

And then she glared at me. "Am not!" She still looked like a small, scared child, but one about to have a tantrum.

Another step, and then I could see clearly into the gloom. Sarah held an armful of stuff she must have taken off the desk or the bookshelves: framed certificates for Rabbi Ellen; what looked like a plaque; a small clear glass trophy. All things that had gone to Rabbi Ellen to celebrate all she'd done over her life, her career. "Put that down," I demanded.

Sarah shrugged. "I'm happy to."

I realized my mistake as she opened her arms . . . and everything in them fell. I lunged, but not in time to keep glass from shattering. It sparkled all around me in jagged shards that would've been beautiful if I hadn't known what they were. Sarah laughed as I backed up as carefully as I could, managing to avoid stepping on any of it. "Now what should I break next?" she asked, tapping her chin as she surveyed the rest of the room. Could she read in the dark? "I see we've got some nice family photos. Some ancient-looking prayer books. They could make a nice . . . blaze."

And then I realized she was holding a book of matches. All the breath went out of my lungs. Somehow I managed to wheeze out some words. "Don't do this, Chana-Lotte."

She sneered at me from the shadows. "Try and stop me."

I had only a split second to think about it. And then I lunged again, this time at her. I was careful to avoid the glass on the floor, not wanting either of us to get cut, which meant that I slammed her sideways into one of the bookshelves. She shrieked with rage as she hit it. A book tipped from the top shelf and fell, narrowly missing her head. "Stop it!" I shouted as we grappled, our arms scrabbling at each other. I yelped as she grabbed a fistful of my hair. "You're hurting me! You're hurting Sarah! You're hurting all of us!"

"Good!" she yelled, and, with a supernatural strength, she shoved me backward. I staggered across the room, nearly hitting the desk. "You deserve it!"

And she turned tail and ran back out the door. I blinked in surprise, but followed just in time to see her kick Gus out of the way, making him roll into the backyard. Maybe this was a good thing? I mean, not for Gus, but for me and Rabbi Ellen? Could the dybbuk be giving up? Again, I got only a split second to hope.

She was still holding the matchbook. She darted to the side so that she was up next to Rabbi Ellen's house, leaving me wheeling clumsily after her, and pulled out a match. "Don't come any closer," she said, holding it in front of her.

And then I noticed the jug of gasoline. The jug of gasoline lying on its side, empty. How had I not noticed the smell before? "Oh my God," I said, my stomach roiling. "What did you do?"

The dybbuk shrugged. "I needed a plan B in case I wasn't happy with what I did inside. And what do you know?" Her eyes darkened. "*I'm not happy.*"

Her fingers twitched, like she was going to light the match. All my insides froze. I had to do something. But what?

Anger hadn't worked. Fighting hadn't worked. Maybe . . . there was another way.

I knew her name now. I knew what she wanted. I glanced over at Gus. What had it said online? That the dybbuk would leave the body at peace when its purpose was fulfilled? Maybe I could do this. Maybe I wouldn't need Gus after all.

I took a deep breath. "I was wrong. I'm not angry at you for trying to help Sarah. It's just that she doesn't need your help anymore," I said gently. "You said you wanted to help Sarah by helping her rebel and by getting revenge on those who'd wronged her. But what if Sarah was happy the way she was? Sarah likes school. She likes keeping kosher. I think she even likes cooking. Keeping kosher and cooking might have been oppressive for you, but not for her. Not everybody needs to do a certain thing to be happy. Everybody is different."

"You're wrong," the dybbuk said, scuffing her toe against the grass. "You don't know anything." Her eyes flashed. "Sarah wants to study Torah, not be at the mercy of your terrible grandmother all the time."

Her hands moved so quick I could barely see them. A sound like sandpaper scraping, and then the match was lit, the little flame jumping cheerily above her fingers. My breath caught in my throat. Now I couldn't even tackle her again, because if she dropped that match . . .

I had only one chance to get this right. A few seconds before everything went boom.

Literally.

I took an even deeper breath, trying to suck in a bunch of courage with it. "I know. You were mad that Rabbi Ellen wouldn't stand up for Sarah. Maybe Sarah *does* need someone to help her and stand up for her." Like I did. Like maybe we all did. "And that someone's going to be me. I'm going to help her. To be there for her."

And just like that, I meant it, way down deep in my bones.

"Yeah? And what about me?"

"You, Chana-Lotte, have achieved your purpose," I said. For some weird reason, tears stung the corners of my eyes. This poor girl. The world had never even found out what happened to her. "You helped Sarah. You got to rebel and live life the way you wanted for a bit, but now it's time to let Sarah live *her* life the way she wants to. And

I'm going to be here to help Sarah stand up for herself and live her life however she wants."

She looked at me for a long time. The match trembled in her hand. "Do you promise?"

When I spoke, it felt like I could hear the chorus of generations behind me, pious Jews all the way back. "I promise." And then I froze, holding my breath. The flame on the match danced, drawing ever closer to her fingers. This was all I had. If this didn't work, things were about to get very painful.

But I didn't step back.

Sarah's eyes glowed red. She gave a jerk, like the one you make when you're falling asleep and think you're falling off a cliff. Then blinked.

Was that Sarah? Was it over?

She raised the match . . .

. . . and blew it out.

I exhaled every drop of air in my lungs, my whole body sagging in relief. I staggered, almost falling over. "I did it."

"You did it," Sarah said. It *was* her again; I could hear it in her voice. She shook out her arms, rolled her shoulders back, cracked her neck. "It feels so good to be in control again. I can't even tell you . . ." She trailed off, shuddering as she rubbed her arms up and down.

"I'm glad you're back," I said, and it was true. I was. No matter how perfect she was. It didn't matter. She could be as perfect as she wanted. If I wanted to change, that was on me. Except when it came to Grandma Yvette. I could control what I did, but not what other people thought of me. And that would have to be enough.

"Listen, Ruby." Sarah paused, wrinkling her nose at the smell of gasoline. At least, I hoped it was the gasoline and not me. "Everything I said that last time we managed to drive the dybbuk off for a little bit? I meant it. All of it."

That already felt like so long ago. "Me too," I said. She stepped forward and wrapped her arms around me. She was warm. I let her hug me, even though I wasn't sure how things would change. "And I meant what I said just now, too. I'm here for you, however you need me. Like, in friendship. And also with Grandma Yvette."

Grandma Yvette. Right. She was waiting in her car, ready to come charging after us.

I disentangled myself from Sarah's arms, stepping back. "Let's take Gus back to Grandma's car," I said. I stooped to pick up Gus, who was still lying on the ground, his arms caught beneath him. I was glad I hadn't had to shove the dybbuk into him. That she could be free. I draped him over my shoulders, staggering again under his weight.

Suddenly the weight lightened. I almost screamed. Gus was alive!

But I turned to see Sarah supporting Gus with one of her shoulders, too.

That was how we walked Gus back to Grandma Yvette's car. Balanced between us, carried on our shoulders, both of us stooping like we were soldiers carrying our wounded comrade off the battlefield.

As soon as we rounded the corner and caught Grandma Yvette's car in our sights, she rushed over. She met us in a cloud of cigarette smoke and perfume. I coughed, readying myself for an enveloping hug, but she pushed me aside, pulling Sarah and Gus into her arms instead. "I knew you'd be back," she said to them, her face in their hair. "Ruby put some ideas in my head, let me tell you! But you look great."

Sarah wasn't hugging her back, just standing there with her arms limp at her sides. That was odd.

Gus wasn't hugging her back, either. That was not odd.

Grandma Yvette went on. "We'll drop Ruby off on the way home, and then how about we have an old-fashioned sleepover, hmm? You look like you could use some of Grandma's famous matzah ball soup."

I bit back a sigh. So we were back to the way things were, then. Sarah would be the golden child again, and I wouldn't just be the silver child, I'd be all tarnished and rusty like I'd been left in the basement for a million years.

I told myself it didn't matter. That my own self-awareness and my own confidence were enough. I didn't need Grandma Yvette's approval. It didn't matter if I was always second.

I was totally lying.

Sarah ducked out from under Grandma Yvette's arms. She looked over at me. I looked mutely back. She swallowed so hard I could see the rings of her throat go up and down, and then turned back to Grandma, who was still clutching Gus like he was holding her up.

"Ruby is the best person I know. The bravest person I know," Sarah said. I blinked. Wait, what? "You don't treat her right, and that's not right, but she's not the one missing out because of that. *You're* the one missing out."

A cold wind hit the back of my throat. Oh. My mouth was hanging open. I shut it with a snap, which made my head reel. Or probably it wasn't just that. It was Sarah's words, too.

She was standing up for me. She was choosing me.

Grandma Yvette shook her head. "That's absurd," she said. "You're not being . . ." But she trailed off, and her mouth opened and closed a few times. "You're imagining things," she finally said. "I love you both. You're both my granddaughters. If I treat you differently, it's because you're different people."

Sarah's face fell. And now it was my turn to stand up for her. I squared my shoulders. "No, Sarah's the best person *I* know," I said. "And you might not treat me right, but you don't treat *her* right, either. She's her own person. If she wants to study Torah at Junior Sisterhood instead of cooking with you sometimes, then that's her right."

I turned to Sarah and held out my arm. She linked her elbow through mine and gave me a firm nod as I turned back to Grandma Yvette. It was Grandma Yvette's turn now to have her mouth hanging wide open in shock.

"If Grandma would rather not have you over, we can go to my house," Sarah told me. "Let's go." She paused and blinked at Grandma Yvette. "By the way, if you want your candlesticks back, they're still up on the roof. I don't want them anymore."

Grandma Yvette's jaw dropped, but neither Sarah nor I said anything else. Together, we got back in the car.

CHAPTER TWENTY-FOUR

OVER THE NEXT FEW MONTHS, I kept expecting everything to slide back into its old routine. For Sarah to glance at me sidelong for not getting Grandma Yvette's approval. For Grandma Yvette and Sarah's Ruby-free sleepovers to resume.

But what Sarah said stuck. Which shouldn't have surprised me, because even Sarah's vows were perfect. She said she wanted to take a break from Grandma Yvette's for a while. Well, after she got done being grounded. She was grounded for ages. It wasn't like she could tell her parents it hadn't been *her* doing all those things.

I think she secretly found being grounded kind of thrilling, actually. She'd never been grounded before.

When I told my parents Sarah wouldn't be at Grandma Yvette's anymore, they said I didn't have to go either if I didn't want to. But even though we were twelve, Sarah's parents didn't think she was ready to be left alone after school every day after all that she did, and they didn't want to pay for daycare.

My parents didn't have to worry about me, because I'd started the shadowing program at the hospital twice a week. I did indeed get to follow Dr. Solomon in the emergency medicine department, seeing what he did and taking notes on whatever he asked me to. I got to see him stitch up a lot of bad cuts, and put emergency tubes into people's mouths and throats and chests, and once even perform CPR until a basically dead person came back to life.

It was the best job ever.

But back to Sarah. She'd joined the art club with Jamilah, and the two of them had gotten really tight. Together they'd even worked on the sets for Aubrey's play.

My mom's car screeched to a halt in front of Sarah's house. The seat belt kept me from smashing my head against the dashboard. I went to text Sarah that we were here, but the front door was already opening and closing. Of *course* she'd been waiting for—

No, I told myself firmly. *Stop that. It's polite of her not to keep us waiting.*

She jogged down the driveway in her spotless maroon sweater and jeans. Her face split open into a smile as she saw me. Her hair swung loose around her face, freed for the night from its usual ponytail.

It came slowly, but she was slightly less perfect than she'd been before. Sometimes she wore her hair down. Sometimes she stayed up late and made videos with me or just hung out when she slept over at my house instead of planning out activities. Like me, she'd learned that there were more important things in life than how people saw you.

And in Junior Sisterhood, she'd really stepped up. After apologizing profusely to Rabbi Ellen for everything she'd said and done as the dybbuk, she'd proven herself smart, insightful, and a born leader. The rest of us suckers had actually just voted her in as president of the club. Unanimously. Which meant probably more studying Torah than I'd prefer, but I was okay with that.

Grandma Yvette had tried to throw her weight around once and drag her back to the kitchen. But I'd stood up next to Sarah and said that we needed her here, and then all the other kids did, too. Even Rabbi Ellen said that surely Grandma Yvette could wait (I figured she'd probably talked to Sarah's mom and gotten her permission to stand up to Grandma Yvette). She hadn't dared show her face there since.

"Did you bring the flowers?" I asked before she got into the car.

She whipped her hands around her back to reveal the huge bouquet of red roses and white baby's breath. "Got them!"

"Good," I said. I wouldn't mention that I'd been envisioning something a lot more casual, colorful daisies or something. Sarah had her own way of doing things, and I had mine, and that was okay. "Hop in." Aubrey would be thrilled either way.

Sarah and I talked the whole drive to school. We talked about Joey Ramirez's new haircut (stupid-looking), how we thought the play was going to go (standing ovations, multiple), what homework we had to do over the weekend (too much). My mom waved us off in front of the school, telling us to tell Aubrey to "break a leg," since apparently saying "good luck" was actually bad luck in the theater.

I'd stopped by after school one day to hear Aubrey sing (spectacular) and admire Sarah and Jamilah's sets (amazing). She was really good at painting and knew how to do shading and blending and all the stuff that made it so that when you were looking at the set and kind of let your eyes cross a little, it appeared to be a real castle in France.

While visiting, I'd flicked some paint on Sarah. It spattered her nose, like blue freckles. She gasped, and for a moment I worried I'd overdone things, because the old Sarah would've freaked out.

But she didn't just grin once she saw it was me, she threw paint at me, too! Which started a paint war. If you look really closely at the background of Belle's village as the eighth grader playing her wanders through with her nose in a book, you can see some spatters of red and blue and gold in the corners of the sky. Fireworks.

Aubrey ran up to us as soon as we walked into the auditorium. Sarah shoved her flowers behind her back just in time. "Don't you have to be backstage?" I asked her.

"In a minute! I just wanted to say hi!" she gasped. I assumed she'd been running everywhere. Which must've been hard in her feather duster costume, which was just as feathered and glittery and elaborate as she'd imagined. She and I had spent an entire weekend at Aubrey's house sewing each little feather onto the floor-length dress Aubrey's parents had bought at the thrift store. "Everybody keeps telling me how amazing I look in this dress! Okay, I'd better go." Despite her costume, she leaned forward and gave me a squeeze. Her feathers pricked me, but I squeezed back. When she backed off, she didn't just leave. She hugged Sarah, then left.

Sarah turned to me, her face glowing. "Okay, I'd better go find Jamilah. I said we'd meet up with her before the show."

"Didn't I tell you you'd like her?" I'd been right, as (not to brag) I so often am. Whenever I stopped by Art Club, I'd find the two of them immersed in heated conversation about different kinds of paint, or some long-ago moment they'd researched after it got a mention in history class, or the intricacies of Jewish dietary law versus Islamic dietary law. I was glad they'd become such good friends, like me and Aubrey. It didn't mean that Sarah and I couldn't be friends again, too. We could grow up and branch out without falling apart.

Over Sarah's head, I saw Rabbi Ellen walking through the doors, herding her grandkids along. Sarah turned to look, too. We both waved. She waved back.

"I want to be like her one day," Sarah said.

"She is a good person," I agreed.

Sarah turned back to me. "No, not just like her. I mean, like, a rabbi." Uncertainty creased her face.

It smoothed out as I said, "I think you'll be great."

Sarah waved down Jamilah, and then the three of us found our seats in the third row, so close we'd be able to see the sweat glittering on Aubrey's face. I said as much to them, and they giggled. "Gross," said Sarah.

"Maybe she'll even spit on us a little," I said.

They giggled even more, and Sarah said, "Gross*er*."

I put my arm on the armrest between me and Sarah. She put her arm on it, too, and for a second we jockeyed over the space, the smiles on our faces enough to show that we were joking. As the lights dimmed overhead, she grabbed my hand so that we were sharing the armrest half and half.

She squeezed my hand. I squeezed back as the red curtain swept open.

I was so excited to see what would happen next.

AUTHOR'S NOTE

There are a lot of variations in the mythology of the dybbuk, and I took the liberty of choosing the ones that worked best for this story and these characters. While most elements of the dybbuk in this book are taken from Jewish mythology or folkloric literature, the concept of the dybbuk box is not; it's more of a modern invention and is not consistent with historical interpretations of the dybbuk, which had to possess something living in order to exist. I hope the ancient sages and historians will forgive me! If you are interested in learning or reading more about the dybbuk, there are many other stories, TV shows, plays, and movies that feature them that you can check out.

Writing and publishing a book truly takes a village.

Thank you again to my agent, Merrilee Heifetz; her assistant, Rebecca Eskildsen; and everybody else at Writers House. Never enough thank-yous to my editors, Mekisha Telfer and Jen Besser, and everybody else at Roaring Brook Press who helped turn this story from a Word document into a book, including Hayley Jozwiak, Avia Perez, Liz Dresner, Susan Bishansky, Kathy Wielgosz, Susan Doran, and Veronica Mang. Special thanks to Olivia Chin Mueller for bringing Ruby to life on the book jacket. And thank you so much to Alix Kaye and Sam Panitch for your insightful critiques that made this a better book.

I named Ruby and Aubrey's teacher Mr. Zammit after a science teacher I had in middle school who told me he thought I would become a psychologist when I grew up because he felt like I was analyzing him and everything around me all the time. Surprise! I was! Thanks for making me feel seen, Mr. Zammit, and for your great name. I'm glad every day that I get to use all of those observations to write books about being in middle school.

As always, thank you to my husband, Jeremy Bohrer, for the endless love and support.